MIN EUROZAN
THE ELORCUIAN CHRONICLES BOOK ONE

MIN EUROZAN
THE ELORCUIAN CHRONICLES BOOK ONE

CATHY JACKSON

Cover design: Stephen Zimmer

Cover art in this book copyright © 2021 Stephen Zimmer & Seventh Star Press, LLC.

Editor: Holly Phillippe

Published by Seventh StarLight, an imprint of Seventh Star Press, LLC.

ISBN Number: 978-1-7362781-9-2

Seventh Star Press

www.seventhstarpress.com

info@seventhstarpress.com

Publisher's Note:

Min Eurozan is a work of fiction. All names, characters, and places are the product of the author's imagination, used in fictitious manner. Any resemblances to actual persons, places, locales, events, etc. are purely coincidental.

Printed in the United States of America

First Edition

Acknowledgements

I want to thank God for this novel. Without Him, this story wouldn't be. I thank Him for teaching and leading me every day.

Matthew Jackson, my amazing husband, thank you for everything. You are my heart and life.

Connor, Ian, Jessa, and Joseph, you are all my joys and loves. It's a privilege to be your mother. I love you so much.

Stephen Zimmer and Holly Marie Phillippe, your faith and belief means more than either of you will ever know. Thank you so much for taking a chance with this book and me.

Christine Feehan and Gena Showalter, thank you for following your dreams and writing the books you love. Your inspiration motivates me every day to be a better writer.

Jennifer Harshman, Annabelle Garcia, and Caprice Whitmire, you continue to play such a beautiful part in my life. Everything you've done, and do, is appreciated.

John Wells, John Thomassen, Tom Proctor, Martin Lopez, and Matthias, I wouldn't be where I am without you. Your kind hearts, generous natures, and motivational work ethics encourage me to be more than I am.

Foreword

Min Eurozan began as a nineteen thousand word short story, but soon took on a life of its own. Judin, Thomael, Kinim, Jaad, Jerren, and Roenn came alive on the page, and it compelled me to record the continuing details of their lives. Every aspect pulled me into the world they inhabited with an insight to their thoughts and actions. I realized it was a privilege to write every triumph and success, along with the defeat and failure. The words fell onto page after page in complicated and messy and joyful and happy ways. They stunned me with every new word, and I was hooked. I had started Min Eurozan in September and finished the manuscript in February. In five short months, I had written over three hundred thousand words and their story was complete.

For Mom

CHAPTER ONE

The Arrival

*W*aking up, my eyelids gently raise to the blue sky, with its fluffy white clouds above me. I can feel the heat from the suns shining down on my body.

Looking at the sky I notice there are two suns. Why is it not hotter than it is?

The ground is warm beneath my back. I feel the hardness of it, holding me up securely.

What time is it?

Placing my hands on the ground I start to rise. Nope, not going to happen. The feeling of vertigo hits me, as I lie back down.

I don't remember laying down in the brown grass. Wait, brown grass?

I touch it and it feels dry. Where am I?

A wave of nausea hits me, as I try to remember where I am or how I got here. It feels like I am being barred from knowing where I am. Why?

Too many questions, and not enough answers. My head begins to ache, as I glance to the blue sky, with wispy white clouds again. There are no vapor trails in the sky. The two suns, one of each side of me, are shining brightly but they aren't too hot. The temperature is just right.

This is weird.

I look around me. Really peer around me to see what is around.

There are mountain ranges on either side of me. I hear water trickling somewhere nearby. There are rocks of all sizes around me. There are small trees, like full grown ones, but smaller dotted around me in a circle. As I turn my head I note the trees are in a perfect circle around me and the vegetation outside the circle is green and lush.

Okay, more normalcy.

Why can't I remember how I got there?

Pushing myself to sit up, the vertigo hits me. I sit quickly and push away the spinning. It takes a bit, but soon it's gone.

"You've acclimated." A familiar male voice in my head, whispers. Strangely, I'm calmed by it. Reassured.

Acclimated? Acclimated to what?

When I close my eyes, I "see" images behind the lids. It's not a memory or my imagination but like a screen brought down. I marvel at what I behold.

Earlier…

"It's going to take some getting used to." His dark brown eyes shifted around me, while I watched him. His hands were tucked into his dove grey cargo pants. I hated it when he was nervous. No matter what situation we are in, it always ended badly when he was nervous.

But my trust in him overrode the fear that had risen in me. "How long?"

His eyes shifted back to mine and he grazed the ground with his Vans. The tops of the grass moved under his shoes. "This is your new home." He cleared his throat, as his Adam's apple bobbed up and down. His bow shaped mouth slanted down when he looked back to me. Fear was stamped on his face. "Forever." He glanced away again. He took the dark temptation of his look away from me.

"Forever?" I gasped and felt him mentally pull away from me.

His eyes, now almost black, pierced mine, impressing upon me the gravity of the situation.

***

My eyelids slide upwards and the images are gone.

Almost immediately, I know I am missing something really important, but I don't know what it is. It's something that I want, something that I need to be whole. Complete.

The feeling wisps away from me and I risk another glance around.

"I need to head north," I hear myself say out loud. It's as if I memorized what I said and repeating it to myself.

Except, I don't remember memorizing it.

As I stand, another feeling of vertigo hits me and I wobble. Nausea rises again, threatening to spill over my lips.

No, I can't be weak right now. I have to be strong.

I swallow the bile and it burns down my throat.

North. Which way is north?

I close my eyes, trying to remember.

Instead, I "see" a movie, already in motion behind my eyelids.

***

"Follow the suns for a day," he says, nonchalantly flashing a hand back and forth. "You will come upon a city. It will be golden." He glances around nervously again and then back to me.

"But I don't want to do that. I want to stay with you." I move closer to him.

He slides back from me, a little. Barely noticeable, but enough for me to know he does not want me touching him.

For some reason that hurts, not being able to lay a hand on his tanned arm or slide my hand into his grip. I can't feel the soft grey shirt slide against me, as I lean close to him. Those actions have always brought me comfort. Now, I can't do that anymore.

"Someone will find you. Trust them." He looks up to the sky, as I follow his gaze, seeing the two suns.

"You're leaving." I gasp. "And I can't go."

His eyes meet mine, pityingly. I hate that look. I'd seen him give it so many times before, when he knew that he couldn't change a situation. "You have to stay." His smile, I am sure means to calm me, does just the opposite. It's too sad. "But you will be well taken care of."

Taken care of, I am sure that means until you die.

But I don't want to stay here. I want to go with him. Always with him. "Why do I have to stay?"

The corners of his eyes turn down a little again. The sad smile still in place. I hate it when he is sad because it makes me sad too. "Because you have to." He draws closer to me and brings his hand into mine. "And live."

I wanted to feel his warmth. Instead, I feel a coldness, radiate from him. It keeps me from him.

"But I want to go with you."

He eyes the sky again, as did I. "You can't. There's no time." He slips his hand out of mine and takes a piece of my heart with him. He steps into the perfect round brown circle with the trees surrounding it. "When someone finds you, tell them I sent you." His eyes find mine and he holds my gaze. "Live. For me."

For him. He wants me to live for him?

"But I don't..." I start, but he raises a hand, palm out, silencing me. I realize it's a hand I know intimately.

"When this happens, you'll fall asleep." He clears his throat, as if he wants to say more, but doesn't. "When you wake up, head north and live. Understand?"

"I'm not inexperienced." I step into the circle beside him.

"You're not." He raises a hand to my face, his fingertips grazing my cheek, as he starts to phase out of this reality. "You're a bright, capable woman and I..." He stops and looks up.

A bright light begins to descend and swirl around him. As it continues to gain momentum, I should feel the wind from it, but I don't. Instead, a dizziness slams into me and I blink quickly, keeping him in view.

He's leaving! No!!

I can feel the rejection and pain of the swirling wind. It has never rejected me before, but does now.

The light starts to dim, and the vortex of motion begins to swirl upward, away from me. The dizziness pushes me to the ground.

It won't take me, and I don't know why.

I strain to keep my eyes open. In a flash, where he is standing is empty and he is gone.

Darkness pushes me toward a blackness that welcomes me with open arms.

*** *

I open my eyes, turning myself to the right, and begin walking. I have no idea how far I have to go, but I trust that he is honest in what he said. I've always trusted him – implicitly. He's never failed me. Not one time.

Even now, stuck wherever I am, doing what he wants, I trust him. I miss him so much it hurts my heart, but I know that the directions he gave me are true.

And so, I walk, not knowing what I will find other than a golden city.

CHAPTER TWO
The Journey

I walk for what seems like hours. Instead of feeling tired, I feel almost renewed with each step I take. My breaths are cleansing. A newness washing over me and, at the same time, a familiarity. It's as if I am going home.

Except I'm not. I have never been to the place I currently am. Hence, where I am going will be foreign to me. I have no experience with it, other than it is a golden city.

I have never ever seen any place golden in all of our travels.

Our travels. Not my travels. Ours. Who is the "ours"?

In my mind, I know I have travelled with two men. I have gone on adventures with them on separate occasions. I have been … places … with them. When I try to reach for the knowledge of where, it alludes me, as if it is a living thing, running from me.

A pain in my head takes me to my knees. I press a palm against where it hurts the most. It is as if what I want to know is there, but I can't access it.

Or is it that I shouldn't access it?

I close my eyes. A familiar, yet strange scene, begins behind my lids.

***

"She shouldn't know. It would only upset her more." His eyes, the color of turbulent sea, flashes to me and then the other man. The light behind him framing his red hair, catching it on fire. "We don't want her agitated." Tenderness laces his soft tone.

The other man, the one I had seen in my memory "movie" with the dark brown eyes, glances to me and then back to the red headed man. "I agree." Care and concern evident in his tone.

I 'look' around myself and see that I am in a bed, naked. A sheet rests on top of me. I can see the men are fully dressed and standing just outside the bedroom.

I'm in a bedroom? In a bed without anything on, while three men watch me sleep. Why am I okay with this? Why does it seem like I trust them? As if I am theirs.

Another man strides up to them. His blonde head turns to the bed. An ache for me emanates from his sky blue eyes. He takes his time perusing my body and glances to the other two men.

"I shouldn't be here." There is an urgency in his voice.

Desire slams into me. I want the three of them. The blonde haired man. And the one with dark brown hair. And the red head.

"I know that." The dark haired one with the dove grey button down shirt answers, quietly. "But we need to make this decision together. Everything we do now has to be done as one. To maintain consistency."

"Yes." The red haired man, in the soft grey suit jacket with thin black lines crossing it, agrees. He unbuttons the jacket with a right hand in a well-practiced move. That hand slides into his midnight colored slacks front pocket. "For her."

"I need to get back." The cornflower blue sleeveless sweatshirt moves with the blonde as he turns to look behind himself. "She is waiting on me. I told her I wouldn't be very long." His eyes find mine again, hungrily. "Maintaining this distance from her is draining my willpower." He physically turns from me to face the other two men.

The shape of his mouth captures my attention. I love it, and what it can do to me. He has an amazingly hearty appetite.

"I feel the same." The red head spoke, as he glances toward me, with a needy expression. The red haired man speaks again and directs his question towards the man with the brown hair. "She's yours now. What do you want to do?"

Three heads turn toward me now. I am the centerpiece of conversation, but feel like the main course of a dinner. I feel as if they are ready to pounce, ready to devour me. First with their eyes, then their mouths, and then their bodies.

They stare openly lustful at me, simultaneously clearing their throats. Almost as one, the blonde and red head turn back to the dark haired one. The blonde one groans quietly, as the red haired one shifts uncomfortably where he stands.

The dark brown eyes of the man wearing the dove grey shirt, are transitioning to black as I watch. He is moving from me to the men. I am missing his presence most of all. "I will take her there."

The red haired man looks to the blonde and then back to the dark one. "Home?"

"Yes. I will take care of her, keep her safe."

The blonde one growls out loud. He clenches his hands, until they become fists. "Then we won't see her."

I sense he is the possessive one. Of the three of them, he would own me. And, heaven help me, I would let him.

The dark haired one turns to the blonde. "No. Not for a while. But her safety is paramount." He takes a breath and continues. "This hasn't been done before. We didn't know what would happen if we all agreed." The red haired man's gaze shifts from him to me and back again. "Now that it has, she must not be brought to harm."

Three sets of eyes watch me now. Sea green ones that

can churn to the color of a stormy sea. Blue ones that can darken to the color of an overcast day. Maple brown ones that can turn black as the darkest night.

I have seen all the changes in their eyes once upon a time. When we were all together. The best night of my life. The only night I can ever remember truly having them as one.

"I would do anything for her." Reverence rings out in the red haired man's voice. "She is my soul."

Blue eyes flash from one man to another and then to me, as I lie on the bed. "Her body is mine." He turns to the other men, challenging them, while speaking the truth.

"And she has my heart." The dark haired one smiles sadly. It's as if he wants what he cannot have just yet.

The red head eyes me again, hungrily. Of the three of them, I feel he is the patient one, waiting to claim me as his, in the most tender way imaginable.

"We do whatever we have to. I just don't have to like it." The tall blonde one watches me carefully.

"At least you still have her for a time." The red haired man's eyes darken to a violent green as he watches the darker haired one. "We don't have that, do we, Kinim?" He turns to the dark haired one.

Kinim's head turns from me, and I feel bereft. "No, Jerren, I don't. And you have yet to fully know her." His hand dropping carefully on the other's shoulder. "But you will."

How does Jerren not know me? I know, somehow, that we have all lain together. Jerren has to know who I was when we were all together. Didn't he? Am I, in my opinion, that brazen?

As I watch myself on the bed, I know I am that brazen. I want those men, like I need my next breath.

"And you, Kinim, you still have her." Jerren glances to the floor. "For a while longer. Until..."

"Until you get her." Kinim raises his hand, still watching the bed. "Quiet. You'll wake her and she needs her rest." He sighs loudly. "Yes, I do have her and will take care of her." He *turns to Jerren. "Take care of her for me, please."*

Understanding eyes meet — both Kinim and Jerren's. Both want me, almost with an equal passion.

"Of course." Jerren holds out a hand. All three men start moving from the door. "We shall have her again." He glances to me as they move away. "She is as sweet to me as warm honey, and I can't wait to partake of her again."

The three of them nod their heads.

It should be scary, how they all move almost as one. But it isn't. It is beautiful, and comforting. Power exudes from them, and I crave it.

"None of us can." Kinim replies, hastily. "But we shall all wait for the right moment. Agreed, Thomael?" He turns to the blonde haired man.

Thomael nods his head, once. "Yes." The softness of his tone is almost my undoing.

I love all three of them equally.

Was that even possible?

They begin walking away from me, talking in quiet tones.

***

"Are you alright?" A female's voice rings in my ears.

I lie curling up on the ground in a fetal position, trying to block out everything around me. Pain sears at me from every direction.

"I shall get you help." Her voice resounds in my head like a gong. Her footsteps are thunderous in my ears. "I'll be right back."

Tears leak from my eyes. I can't help it. Every sight, smell, and sound around me rings through my body, like knives stabbing at me.

"Please." I beg as I have done on more than one occasion. I don't know what I am begging for, but I need it desperately. "Please."

The pain in my chest magnifies, as I curl into myself

more. Sounds, I know should be indistinguishable to me, rush at me in succession. I can't block them out. The light hurts my eyes. When I try to open them, it is as if daggers are piercing them.

"I don't want to be alone." I wrap my arms around my stomach and cry, until all of my tears are spent.

***

Loud footsteps crunch near me. Booming voices overlap.

"Where does she comes from?" A woman states, her voice tired.

More footsteps, then complete silence.

"We'll take her to the city." Says a man, his voice is controlled, authoritative. He is used to getting what he wants. It isn't a command, but a request. "She is in much pain. We must be silent as we walk. I will tell the others to take care as we move."

"Yes, sir." This is from the worried woman.

More footfalls, this time retreating from me.

"I will take care of you."

The man's voice is soothing, and I begin crying silently.

"I know. You will be well."

I feel his hand hover over my eyes, but he is not touching them.

"Sleep."

As my body begins to relax, I feel a set of hands slipping beneath me, as I am being carefully lifted into a set of man's arms.

Behind my eyelids, I see worlds rotating on their axes. The colors are vibrant and true. I see myself with a blond man, watching the planets, and then with a dark haired man. Thomael and Kinim. I adore Thomael, and see him as my equal. I love Kinim with all of my heart, even though there are times he is too controlling. I think there should be a red haired man, but never see him. Who was he? Had our time not yet come? Was he a figment of my imagination?

I never fully lose consciousness, but lightly rest. Every sound comes to me, but seem as if they have been muted. While I am grateful, I am also curious. How do all of the noises quiet as I am carried to wherever I am being taken? I could have sworn they are loud until we arrive and then hushed.

Who are these people? Why do the arms I am in, feel so familiar, yet strange? Where am I being taken?

Feels we move for quite a while, then stop. I feel as if I am moving up a set of stairs and rising, as if in an elevator. I "see" the dimming and brightening of the light and feel the air moving around me. All of my senses are alert, but I don't want to respond to them.

I know I should be fearful of not being able to react to stimuli, but I'm not. Intuitively, I know the man holding me will take care of me. Of everything. I shouldn't have that complete trust in someone I have just met, but I do. In fact, that has only happened to me once. I don't know when, but know it has. I also know that trust led me here. Wherever here is.

I want to see where I am and who is holding me. So, I am making the conscious choice to open my eyes. They will only peek open, just a little, enough for me to get a good look at the man holding me.

His hair is white and elegantly coiffed. There are lines around his shining eyes and laugh lines around his bow-like mouth. He is tall and standing ramrod straight. An air of confidence and authority surrounding him. His footsteps are sure.

As he speaks, it is for my ears only. "You should be sleeping."

I want to answer him, tell him who I am, and ask him who he is. Tell him I want answers to questions I have. I want to know everything about where I am and what is happening.

But I don't speak.

"You aren't afraid."

Not a suggestion or idea, but a statement of fact. He knows he's right, and that I'm not scared of him.

"I will care for you until you are ready."

Until I am ready for what? And why do I believe everything he has said?

We are still moving, walking up a set of stairs to the top of them. It's just he and I now. I had heard the other footsteps fall away.

I am propped up against a thick stack of pillows and chance a glance around me.

The room is elegantly appointed and huge. A canopied bed in ivory brocade, with a soft comforter. The entire room is done in shades of gold and ivory. A chair sits on both sides of the bed and on the other side of the room sits a large desk. Behind the desk is a golden curtain that stretched from floor to ceiling. A chair sits on both sides of the desk. Between it and myself are several lower tables and a few richly appointed chairs.

Odd that a bedroom and meeting room should be mixed.

The man brushes a thumb across my forehead and speaks quietly. "I will take your pain."

His eyes close and the pain ceases. I see him barely wince. Then he straightens his countenance and withdraws himself from me.

Life comes back to my limbs. I pull myself up on the bed and stare at him. "Who are you? Why do I feel as if I know you? Where am I? Are you going to hurt me?"

He shakes his head once, no hair ever leaving its place. "Please leave us." His glance to the side is quick and then his hazel eyes come back to me.

As I turn to look behind him, I see a man slip out of a door, shutting it behind himself.

"Who is that?"

"Christan. He's my ... confidante." His words are articulate. Measured.

"Confidante?" Something tells me what he is saying isn't

quite true. "And you are?"

"You should be alright now." He holds out his hand. "If ever you need anyone to take the pain away, ask me." This is the first demand he has ever given me.

"Why you?" I'm not about to shake the hand he offers until I am satisfied with his answers.

"I am … special. I am the only one you know now that can heal you from what you experience. I wish you no harm, but to help with whatever you need."

He can't know about me trying to remember the past and the incapacitation that comes with it. "And how would you know what I experience?"

"I don't. Not exactly." He drops his hand and moves across the room to the curtain. "I have an idea who you are, where you came from, and why you were left here." He is almost convincing me with his words.

Left here. I wince at the thought.

"My apologies on the choice of words." He moves to the curtain and opens it quickly. "My name is Jaad and I welcome you to the city of Elorcui."

I come to my knees and touch one of the posts at the end of the bed, as I peer out the window. Spread out in front of me is a beautiful golden city. It is stunning in its artistry and magnificence. Thin spires stand proudly, squat buildings slope and various other structures bow down to a rectangular building that almost touch the clouds. Everything is overlaid in a brilliant gold that gleams in the twin suns. It all looks as if it is on fire.

For some reason, the view makes my heart race. I want to see it all. I want to experience everything the city has to offer. Climb its walls, taste its food, meet the people, and get to know everything about Elorcui.

A reticence makes me draw back. I don't know why or where it is coming from, other than that I don't know anyone in this city. At the same time, it is as if everything I see is familiar. That nothing has changed.

These mixed feelings bring on new feelings of fear. As excited as I am to be here, I have no idea where I am. And that feeling overrides everything else.

CHAPTER THREE
The Unknown

"You haven't answered any of my questions." I tear my eyes from Elorcui and rest them on Jaad. "Why do I feel as if I know you?"

Turning to the window he looks out over the city. "This city has stood for as long as I, my mother, and my grandmother can remember. More than six thousand of your Earth years have passed since its construction. Elorcui stands as a testament to what could be accomplished if we all work together to promote peace."

It is indeed a beautiful city. How has its citizens come to achieve the peace? Why did they need to?

He turns back around to watch me, "You are from Earth."

"Yes." I reply, sliding off of the bed, needing to move. A restlessness has settled over me, along with an energy needing to be exerted. "This is not Earth," I state, watching Jaad.

"You know that already. Earth does not have two suns," he replies, stating the obvious.

I had seen the twin orbs, half the size of the Earth's sun when I awoke. "True." So many questions without answers are flitting through my head. The pain returns and I begin to collapse, crying out.

Jaad catches me, pulling me close. His thumb is touching my forehead. I think I hear a door open, but I am not sure. There is a stabbing pain in my head that consumes me.

***

I find myself standing on a large diamond planet while other diamonds of various sizes stay in perfect formation around us. I am with the blond man – Thomael. He is like a best friend, but so much more.

The sun overhead shines down, a brilliance is cast to all it touches. Colors are everywhere and I marvel at them.

"Why are we here?" I asked, looking to Thomael. "I thought we are going to Dawid. This is place is nothing like you described." I shoulder bump him, playfully. "Did you get us lost?"

Thomael watches the universe around us. He is quiet, and when he is like this, he is thinking of something sad.

I moved to stand in front of him. I loved how the colors play with the blue in his eyes, how his muscular arms feel under my hands, how his body is seemingly always taut – ready for action, how he wears his heart on his sleeve, not revealing it to anyone but me.

He flicks his eyes down to me. I am a full head shorter than him. There is a change in his eyes as they search my face. "Do you trust me?"

"I do. Implicitly." I reply, without hesitation. How can I not? For the last three years, he has given so much to me, that I can't hold back anything from him.

His thick hands grip my rounded shoulders, not bringing me close. Our relationship isn't like that.

I drop my hands.

"No. Stop and think." He takes a deep breath and plunges on. "Do you really trust me?"

I am starting to worry. Not for me, but for him. Desperation drips from his words... Again I can only answer what I know in my soul. "Yes." I grab his arms again. "I trust you with all that I am."

"All that I am", he repeats, shaking his head. His hands slipping from me as he drops to the ground. He brings up his hands to marvel at them. "And that will never change, will it?"

I come to the ground in front of him. "No, never, Thomael. I want to go where you go, love what you love, see what you see. I never want to leave you."

Those ocean blue eyes come to me. "And I would never make the choice to leave you. We've had some fun, haven't we, Judin? Made many happy memories, laughed at ridiculous things, been terrified as we encountered new beings. All of it was with you." He brings one of his hands to my dark blonde hair.

I hated the color of it. My mother always called it 'dishwater blonde' and, to me, that has a negative connotation.

He runs a few strands through his fingers, watching it move. "It's like honey, your hair. All warmth and sunsshine. I could stare at it for hours."

He could? There had never been any indication of his likeness for my hair.

"There is only one time I allowed myself to really feel it in my hands." His eyes finding mine, impressing upon me something. I have no clue what he is trying to convey. "In those few moments, I really knew all there is to know about Judin Lirie." His other hand clutches my upper arm desperately. "I know your touch, taste, and smell. Every secret part of you is what I will keep inside of me. Forever."

What was he talking about? Had we been together, and I didn't remember it? When? How? "What are you talking about?" I am blushing. "We've never..." I replied, glancing off into the distance. He was more like a brother to me. I didn't love him like that.

Leaning closer to me, I feel his warm breath on my face. "Will you kiss me? One last time?"

One last time? But we have never kissed! Tears spring

forth from my eyes, dripping onto my turquoise shirt. "What's going on, Thomael?" I say, as my hands move to bunch in his bright blue sleeveless sweatshirt. He always wears this thing! It is part of who he is. That, and the light blue denim jeans and white Vans. "We've never... kissed. There has never been a first time." I am searching his eyes desperately, trying to understand what he is saying.

"I can't believe you agree. My heart almost stopping in my chest, knowing I can finally have you." He brings me closer to him. "And you are everything I imagined you would be. You bring me more happiness than I ever thought imaginable in this lifetime. Thank you, Judin."

"You aren't making any sense." Tears are flowing freely from my eyes. "What are you talking about?"

Thomael turns his head to the sky. I do too. A bright light has begun funneling down along with a wind. We are standing in the middle of it. As it touches us, Thomael pulls me to him. "We're going home."

I close my eyes, and then reopen them. We are inside a s circle of brown grass surrounded bystones. Trees and mountains are all around us.

We have never been here before.

"Where are we?"

Thomael buries his face in my neck and breathes deeply. Wetness runs down my shirt. Thomael's chest heaves violently. "You trust me implicitly." It is part statement, part question. "Then I ask that you stay here until I return." This was a command. He lifts his face from my neck not moving away from me. Tears glisten in his eyes.

"Where are you going?" I watch as his eyes sweep down my body.

When our eyes met again, he says, smiling. "You are perfection." He sighs loudly. "I guess I don't get that kiss."

I swallow my courage as he moves away from me. Before he can fully rise, I touch his shoulders lightly. He turns from me and looks behind himself. At my touch, he turns back to me.

"What is it?" His fingertips reaching for my cheek.

What am I supposed to say? This was all confusing. Everything since the diamond planet has been one big riddle.

"I'll stay here. For you. But I want something in exchange."

He comes back to me. "Whatever you want. It's yours."

"I want you to kiss me." I never in my wildest dreams imagined asking Thomael to kiss me. But here I am doing so. As I said the words, I knew I want it to happen. More than anything in the history of time, I want to know what it is like to press my lips to his.

I feel the urgency slam into his body. "Really?"

"Yes. But you must do so quickly." I lick my lips, readying for his kiss. It has been a long time since I kissed a man. I hoped I would do it right. For him.

His arms wrap around me, pulling me to him.

I slant myself to his side, ready for him to do what he wants.

"You have no idea how long I have dreamt of this moment," he says, descending to me.

He dreamt of kissing me? That was news to me. He has always treated me like a sister.

At this moment, brotherly thoughts were not running through my mind, but base ideas. I am welcoming him, allowing him to do what he wants to me.

"But it won't be quick, min eurozan. I shall take as much time as I can, and kiss you like I have always wanted to do. And when I am done, you shall want no other man."

Since I had met Thomael, I didn't want any other man. In all of our adventures, visiting other times and worlds, I have never been attracted to any man like I am him. I would be forever his.

His tongue came out to lick his lips and then disappeared back into his mouth. As I am being drawn closer, he takes a deep breath, one of his arms snaking around my back, as I am twisting further to the side. I am in the perfect position to receive his kiss.

Our lips meet and the air comes alive with electricity. My first thought is we are going to be transported again, but that doesn't happen.

I keep my eyes open, watching him stare at me. I want to remember everything about this moment. The way his lips are touching and slanting over mine. The way my mouth opened, before he even had a chance to try and coax it. The feel of our tongues dueling, while I surrender to his searching of my mouth.

His hand finding my neck, fingers closing around it with just enough pressure to keep me in place. His arm behind my back bringing me close enough to be a second skin to him. He is devouring everything about me, oppressing my senses, and dominating all that I am.

And I revel in it. I revel in him, and all that he is. I want to give him everything he asks for, without recompense.

Even as our breaths mingle, I know, if he asks, I will give myself up so that he could live. I have sold my soul to him at zero cost without even realizing it.

In short, I want all of him.

Too soon, my breathing is becoming labored. Bright spots appear in my vision of him. Blackness rims my view. I am losing the oxygen my body needs, but I don't care.

Couldn't care.

He stops kissing me, but not drawing away. He inhales through his nose and exhales into my mouth. I receive the breath and do the same to him. We are literally breathing for, and in, one another. For a time, everything seems to be standing still for us, as we nurture the other.

His hand creeps up my back and cups my head. Our eyes are locked on one another, but I see his as they change from a brilliant blue to the color of a turbulent daytime sky. Anger flashes in them, as he rips his lips from mine.

"Enough." He lets go of me and springs to his feet. "I have to go."

My arm comes up and my hand touches his thigh.

"Don't." My whole body is on fire, alive in areas that hadn't been awakened in a very long time.

He reaches a hand down and touches his fingertips to my face. His digits are soft like butterfly wings. "I can't stay, min eurozan." He looks behind himself and then back to me. "I have to leave. But if I could stay, it would be only to have you, and it is not yet our time."

Not yet our time? What does that mean? I furrow my eyebrows, trying to reason what he is saying.

He moves back to me. His other hand touching the left side of my face. "I know that you do not fully understand what I mean, but you will. One day." He leans down at the waist searching my eyes. "I shall return. Wait for me here."

With that, he turns and strides purposefully away from me.

Where is he going? When will he return?

I settle in where he has left me and began the waiting I promised him I would do. I look up to see two suns in the sky.

Impossible!

**

As I begin to regain consciousness, I feel the piercing pain. Jaad begins speaking quietly. "I will take your pain." Opening my eyes, I see his closing and the creases around his eyes are straining. He now opens them and is watching me. "You are better."

"Yeah. My head isn't hurting anymore." I am laying down on the floor in Jaad's arms. "How do you do that?" I say, dropping my elbows to the floor and Jaad withdrawis his arms from me. He begins walking over to the desk, he doesn't stand behind it, but to the side.

"You already know who I am, but won't admit it to yourself. Not yet. You're not ready to know. But when you do, you won't be surprised for it is why you trust that I will care for you."

I stand now and draw myself up to my full height. Still much shorter than Jaad. "I'm on a foreign planet somewhere in time with people I don't know yet, but do feel that I know, for some reason understand. And you give me more riddles? Really, Jaad? At some point I'm going to need some answers." I say, bringing my hands to my ample hips.

Jaad looks me straight in the eyes. "Please, for your sake, don't look for them. You may hurt yourself. All will be known when it needs to be."

"More riddles. More unanswered questions." I shoot back at him. I'm not usually this emotional, but I can cheerfully throttle the man in front of me.

He moves slowly to me, careful not to disrupt the space around me. "You don't blindly trust many people, and that is good. But you do me."

Again, not a question. "Yes. And I don't know why." I am holding back a tremble at his presence. There is something about him that makes me fully alert.

"You're not afraid of me." He says, taking a step forward, maintaining eye contact.

"No," I say, clasping my hands in front of me. "I just met you and I really don't know what to think of you. Other than your name, I don't know who you are." Raising my head I glance around the room again. "This place is nice, but I don't understand why you brought me here."

"Do you think I have anything nefarious in mind for you?" He states, taking another step toward me and then stopping.

I watch him. If he had wanted to do anything, he already had plenty of opportunity. "No. I just don't understand why I am here," I say, sweeping the room with my hand.

He takes another step toward me and stills. If he chooses, he can touch me. "You are to be my guest. For a little while."

"Guest?" My left eyebrow lifts. Not realizing I have been backing up as he has been moving forward, the back of my knees touch the bed. "As in, I can't leave this room?"

"You shall. When I deem it safe. Until then you will

remain here." He nods and I glance in that direction. Christan is standing at the door. Beside him is a button, the same color as the wall, flat and recessed, about seven foot off the ground. He's tall and doesn't have to strain to reach it. He presses it, but I don't notice a difference.

"What just happened?" I say, watching Jaad and barely noting the city gleaming behind him. "What did Christan do?"

"It is for your protection. Nothing will happen to you, if I can help it. Christan and Janele are the only ones who know about your presence in the city."

"Why?" I ask, deliberately. This feels too familiar to me, like I have been in a situation similar to this before.

"We don't have visitors." He states, flatly. His tone tells me to let it go, but I can't.

"You don't have visitors?" I peer beyond him, out the tall window. "Elorcui doesn't have visitors? Why?" I say, glancing back to Jaad again. "Then how do I...?" I allow my question to trail off. It feels as if Jaad won't divulge the information to me, no matter how much I ask.

I'm right. He watches me but doesn't offer to fill in the blanks of my mind.

"Fine. I was brought here, but by who?" I don't want to close my eyes, but I feel them starting to drop.

I feel the rushing of sound and pain threatening to overwhelm me. I know it will debilitate me, so I drop to my knees, waiting.

"No!" Jaad's booming voice rings through the room.

The sound and promise of pain recede, fleeing from the voice.

"How do you do that?" I ask, marveling.

Jaad nods at Christan who pushes the button again. He moves forward and brings himself to his knees in front of me. His hands wrap carefully around my wrist and he pulls my hands from my face.

I didn't realize I had put them there.

"You will be given every comfort, anything you desire,

everything you need is at your disposal. All you need do is ask." He brings my wrists together and stares at where they are joined. "All I ask in return is that you try not to remember. Not until I say it's safe to do so. Every time you do will only bring you pain, and I don't want to see you hurt. Ever." He leans forward, toward where he has lightly clamped my wrist together with his hands, then moves swiftly backwards, lowering his hands. "Forgive me. I lost myself in you for a moment."

Lost himself in me? My eyes widen as I glance to him. Does he desire me? No. No! No!!

Standing, he nods to Christan who pushes the button on the wall again. "Calm. Calm." Bringing out one of his hands, palm up, he begins to push it forward.

Instantly, I feel a blissful peace. I am still angry, angrier now that he has taken my will away from me.

"It shall not happen again." His tone is resolute. "You are confused, and tired. Tell me what you would like."

His voice is coaxing me to tell him the truth. "I want to rest, and I am afraid of what I do not know."

He moves back to the bedroom area, but he does not enter it. "Know this, Judin Lirie, nothing will befall you while you are with me. I shall make sure of it."

I feel a compulsion to go the bed and lay down on it. But first, I want a shower and clean clothes.

"If you make your way to the door to the left of your bed, you will find a fully stocked closet and relief area. Once you are refreshed, you should try sleeping. I will have your heart's desire brought to you when you are ready. Until then, I will lift a screen. You will see me, but I won't see anything in your room, not until you make it so. Feel free to move about. I will be here when you need me."

Turning from my sight he moves to the big desk. Several monitors appear, hovering just above the desk. They are see- through and displayvarious types of information. Jaad focuses on the displays, touching them in rapid succession, immersing himself in his work.

I am a bird in a gilded cage. A lavish room with the promise of anything I want surrounds me, yet I am still a prisoner. I am trapped. For now, there is nothing I can do, but wait. My time will come and I will break free. If I have to make it happen, any way I have to, I will. I intend to not be kept here very long.

CHAPTER FOUR
The Discovery

J move to refresh myself as Jaad had suggested. Opening the door to what he said is the closet area, I see a huge closet stocked with everything I could ever want in attire and accessories. On the other side of the closet is a large bath that includes a walk-in shower without walls or a door, a large tub that I can walk into, a lengthy double sink with storage space underneath, once again filled with all that I might need, and an enclosed toilet area. The room is decorated in ivory and gold. Bath and hand towels are readily available along with washcloths. Nothing in this room has been overlooked. Even various bath beads, soaps, and fizzes are arrayed in abundance. There is even a body warmer between the shower and tub. An in-wall warmer that is stocked with towels and washcloths too.

Locking the door while I am undressing, I lay the clothes in a chute next to the door. Closing the lid, making my way to the shower and bath, I enjoy a much needed freshening up. Finishing, I begin to wrap myself in a warm towel and start drying off.

In my closet I notice a floor length dressing gown with long sleeves. A pink ribbon sits daintily in the middle of it. As I am dressing, I feel the silkiness of it flowing over my body, and it makes me feel pretty.

Back into the bathroom I go, brushing my teeth and combing my hair until it is dry.

Walking back to my bed, I sit and watch Jaad talking and working with others. None of them look my way. I wonder if they can see me. Jaad had said no, but still.... I begin waving my arms up and down, but no one acknowledges me. Maybe they can't see me?

After a while, the room on the other side fills with people. The suns have set and the city glows fluorescently. Is the gold a conductor for the light during the day, storing it for use at night? That would be clever. But what would they do on days that it is overcast? Is there a holding station somewhere?

Jaad glances my way as I yawn. Suddenly, I am very tired. The day must have caught up with me.

A great pulsing ache starts in my head and a searing pain rakes my entire body. I whimper, squeezing my eyes tightly shut, then curl up on my side falling immediately to sleep.

I'm asleep, but the memory doesn't care. It doesn't wait for me to regain consciousness. It takes me anyway.

***

I was sitting in the stone circle, waiting. At some point, I think I have fallen asleep, but don't remember doing so. When I roused, I see a man walking toward me. He's a little taller than I. His dark, brown curly hair is combed back on top and short on the sides. A smile graces his good looking face, but I don't know him. Was he from this place? Does he know Thomael?

He approaches the circle and steps inside. He brings out a hand and reaches down for me. "Did you have to wait long?"

Moving back from him, but not far, I glance at his hand, then back to him. I told Thomael I wouldn't go anywhere.

"Oh, sorry. I'm Kinim. My apologies for keeping you waiting. Are you ready to go?"

I loved the sound of his voice and he was handsome, but he was not Thomael. "I've promised a friend that I wouldn't go anywhere. He's going to come back for me, and I need to be here."

"Oh." He tilts his head, bringing an arm up and scratching at the back of it. "While you are waiting, want to come with me?"

He seems so eager and ready for fun, but I don't know him.

"No. Thank you." I say, glancing behind him. "I'll wait for Thomael." I look to him. "Do you want me to step out while you..." I begin.

He held up a hand, palm out. "I don't know how to tell you this, but Thomael isn't coming back."

Not coming back? "What happened?"

The man looks around nervously. "It was his time to Become someone new. His thousand was up and he chooses to live."

What does that mean? "You said Thomael isn't coming back and that he is alive." I stand and cross my arms. "Thomael wouldn't leave me here. He said he was coming back, and he will. I'll wait here until he does." I begin staring behind the man, waiting for the one I have spent the last three years with, the one who has put his life on the line for me, the one I have put my life on the line for, the one I have given myself to. "I promised."

His light grey button down shirt blows in the slight breeze as he watches me. "You must love him very much."

I glance to him and then back to where Thomael had gone. "I don't think I did until we..." I trail off. This stranger doesn't need to know that Thomael and I had kissed. That he wanted me, and I would have submitted to him. "Anyhow, when he gets back, he'll clear all of this up. You'll see."

The man's dark eyes move over me and come back to my face. "Does he know how you feel? That you care?"

I wipe at the tears that spring from my eyes. "I didn't

get a chance to tell him. He said he had to leave, but that he would come right back. I am going to tell him then." I say, quietly chuckling. "I should have told him that I loved him. Before he left, I should have said that I loved him."

He crosses his arms and kicked a Vans covered foot over the grass. "How do you think he would have responded... if you would have told him?"

I shake my head. "I don't know. He didn't say he loved me so maybe it is one sided. He said we had been...," Glancing to the stranger, not sure why I was telling him these things, "together. If we had, I would have remembered it. I would have remembered him."

"Maybe you haven't been with him yet?"

I swing my head to him and glare. "How can I not have been with him yet? We have been almost inseparable for three years. I would have known."

"Would you have? Maybe he kept it from you. Did he say anything to suggest something had already happened?" He uncrosses his arms and watches me.

Of all the insufferable! "No." I pause, a memory bubble bursting in my brain. "He said, 'he wanted to kiss me one last time' and that he 'only allowed himself once to really feel my hair in his hands.'" I state, gasping loudly. "Does that mean...? Surely, it doesn't mean...?"

"Did he call you 'min eurozan'?"

Blinking as more tears fall, I can hear him clearly in my mind, speaking to me.

"Did he say that you are 'perfection' and that he has 'dreamt that this moment would happen'?" The man in front of me spoke the words as if they were his, but they weren't. It was very confusing.

"Yes. And that if he could stay, it would be only to have me, and it is not yet our time." Stepping back, I remain in the circle, narrowing my eyes at him. "How long have you been watching us? What planet are you from? If you have done anything to Thomael, I swear I'll..." Throwing myself at him,

he catches me in his arms. Fisting my hands, I beat his chest. "Do you hear me? I'll..." Tilting my head just a little so I look up at him, his midnight eyes catch mine.

I could have sworn they were a dark brown. I stop struggling, curiosity overriding my fear for Thomael.

One of his hands remains wrapped around me as he brings another hand to my hair. He pinches some of the strands between his thumb and forefinger, closing his eyes as he rubs the two fingers together. "It's still like honey, your hair. All warmth and sunshine. I can still stare at it for hours."

I look at his fingers, playing with my hair. "We have only just met. You don't know how it feels."

His eyes never leave my hair. "There were so many planets and each time I swear you change with each new adventure. You are perfect for me. If I believed in a soulmate, she would be you." He looks deep into my eyes. "I wonder if, who I am now, you will still be what I need?"

I am lost. He had said so much that I don't have time to process it all. I should want to move from him, not be in his arms, and be watching out for Thomael.

But I don't want to move from him. I feel right in his arms. "We've never gone to any planets together. I have no idea what you are talking about."

"I watched you, on the diamond planet, as you marveled at the brilliance around you. You shone brighter than any of the diamonds. I wanted to tell you how beautiful you looked, but I didn't dare. I knew my thousand was up and that I had a choice to make."

"What are you talking about?" I incline my head to watch him.

He turns his head to me. "I've been alive so long, you see, that I wasn't sure I wanted to go on. I had a choice. End my cycles, or choose life. When you let me kiss you, and I knew what the future held, I knew I what I wanted." His smile was a wondrous thing to behold. "I want you. The decision is easy. I chose to live. For you."

"What?" I begin trembling, scared of what he will say and of what he won't. "What does all of this mean?"

"This is my second cycle. My name was Thomael and is now Kinim."

Kinim, I like that, I think to myself.

"What do you think? A bit too feminine?"

He was Thomael. Now he is Kinim. My thoughts are trying to keep up with everything.

"Well, do you like it?"

He was waiting for me to answer him. In truth, I liked the name Kinim. And no, it isn't too feminine. "I do."

His laughter was rich. "If my lady approves, then so shall I." Kinim whisks me out of his arms, standing back. "I now present to you, Kinim. The new and improved Thomael." He bows at the waist, standing erect, and laughs. "What do you think of that?"

"Thomael isn't coming back?" I step back to where I started in the circle. "Ever?"

Kinim turns his head to the right a fraction. He brings his hands out in front of him and places them palm side together. "He is me now. Is that a problem?"

The words are said exactly the same way Thomael would have said them. "How did we meet? Thomael and I?"

He brings his hands to his upper arms clasping them. "You had just finished your shift at work and I was watching you. You didn't know but I had been eyeing you for a while. The whole night in fact. I liked how you handled yourself with people, how you really thought about their welfare before your own. You are good with people, and while most don't appreciate it, you don't pay attention to that because you are the embodiment of love. So, like I said, I waited until you were done with work, came up to you, introduced myself, told you who I was and what I did. After you scoffed and called me crazy," he takes my hand in his, "I slid my hand into yours and asked you to come with me." He shook his head. "For some reason, you agreed. We went to a park and played on the swings for hours. I knew you were tired, but you stayed. With me. When you declared it was time for you to go home, we walked there together. I walked you up to your door," he lifts my hand and kisses it exactly like he had that night, "and told you..."

"I would never be alone again." I finish for him. Everything he had said was right.

"That you would never be alone again. I would take care of and protect you. We met for coffee the next day and chatted for hours. It was your day off and you didn't want to leave. Truth be told, neither did I. So, we stayed in the shop until they closed."

"They asked us to leave so they could turn off the lights." I interject.

"You said, you hadn't finished your coffee. So, you upended the cup, drank it all, and sat it down on the table. We left shortly after." He brings my hand down between us, but doesn't let go. "I told you that I want to take you with me since I first saw you. That I wanted to show you people and places and civilizations beyond your imagination. You asked what that meant, and I suggested that I show you."

"And you did." I add, slowly becoming addicted to the feel of his hand in mine.

"You've never let go since." His eyes meet mine, and I couldn't look away.

"Is it painful? Changing?" I don't want Kinim to be hurt for any reason. Any more than I want Thomael to feel discomfort.

"Yes." His other hand slips into mine. "But I knew, when it was all over, I was coming back to you. I would crawl through the flames to come back to your side."

"You're really him?" It was almost too impossible to believe. But this man – Kinim – knew tiny details about my life with Thomael. His feelings and gestures, even mannerisms, show me that this was indeed Thomael. Just not how I had seen him last.

"I'm really him." His grin was infectious. I can't help but smile back at him.

I accept that. "You're going to have to be patient with me. You don't look like him or talk like him or act like him. It's going to take some getting used to."

"I shall be patient." His right eyebrow shoots up. "And you? What will you do if you can't 'get used to' me?"

For some reason, I don't think that is possible. "The question, dear sir, is what will you do if we aren't compatible, you know, because of who you are now?"

"I don't think that will be a remote possibility." He slips one of his hands out of mine and arcs it across his head. He is looking back at me, still smiling. "Don't ever think that there will ever be a time that I won't need or want you because that time will never be."

His statement was serious, and I love his smile. Everything about him seems new, and old, at the same time. He is all that Thomael was and more.

"Where to now, sir?" I ask, waiting for him to decide.

One of his hands is still in mine as we both look up. I move to his side, anticipating our next trip. All he has to do is think of where he wants to go, and we will be there.

"How about to the stars, madam?" He lays a hand over mine.

"Yes, please." I eagerly welcome our next adventure!

***

I cry out loudly in my sleep. The pain is almost unbearable. Consciousness is slipping from me. I'm not safe from it even in my slumber.

"I'm here. Calm."

I'm gathered up into arms that I am becoming way too familiar with. They are his – Jaad's. I feel his thumb on my forehead. "I will take your pain."

The prickling begins to leave my body. I feel it begin to

pass to Jaad.

He holds me tighter in his arms, but doesn't say anything. His will tries to dominate mine. I feel the 'push' and submit to it. Now that my body is free of what is threatening it, I look at him. His eyes are shut tight and there is a slight wince. He opens them, takes a deep breath, and is peers down at me. "Are you alright now, dear?"

Dear? His concern is apparent as he watches me. I am nothing to him – a stranger – who he chooses to keep captive in an opulent cell.

"It's alright now." I reply, cautiously.

He cradles me in his arms like a China doll. Like I am some precious thing. I have never been anyone's China doll.

Have I?

Pieces of beautiful moments are skirting my mind but don't surface. Times I should remember, but ones that don't allow me to.

"They come to me, like a dream. A cream I want to remember but can't. I know I want that dream to be real. It is like it isn't a dream at all, but really happened. And I want those times back, but they are shut out to me. I can't access them because they are blocked or something." I have said all of this in desperation. I'm not sure what I'm not being allowed to see, but I know they are wonderful and exciting. A part of me has been locked away from myself and I want it back!

"You have too long to go to be remembering anything, my dear." Jaad turns me to face him. My eyes come to his hazel ones and I am falling hard into them. "This time when you rest, you shall not dream, but wake refreshed." His hand comes up and sweeps down. "Sleep."

My eyelids drop and I feel a strong 'push' in my mind from Jaad. My body immediately goes under and I am instantly asleep.

CHAPTER FIVE
The Outing

I sleep hard, but awaken ready for the day. I think something has happened during the night, but I can't remember what it is.

Jaad is still in his office, working and talking. New people coming and going. Through it all, he never falters.

My stomach rumbles. I would kill for a stack of warm vanilla pancakes with real maple syrup and bacon. Yeah, that would hit the spot. I am not sure when I have last eaten.

A knock sounds at the door and Jaad moves to answer it. He takes the tray from someone behind the door and comes over to my room. He sits the tray down on a low table and goes back to the crowd.

"Please forgive me everyone, but I need a time of respite. I should be ready to continue working in an hour. We shall meet back here then."

At that, everyone gathers their things and exits the room. All but Christan, who is standing by the door.

Jaad nods to him and Christan copies his expression.

"Good morning, dear," he says, picking up the tray and standing patiently. "If I may. Breakfast."

"You may. Good morning."

Christan pushes the button and Jaad comes into the

room, smiling. "I trust you slept well." He begins setting the food and drinks on a table with two padded chairs on either side.

I can't get over the ostentatiousness of the room. "I think so." The smell of the food hits me and I want to weep. "Pancakes and bacon?" I ask, walking over to the food. "And real maple syrup?" I can't wait to sit down and dig into my food.

Jaad finishes arranging it all and pulls out my chair. "My lady."

"Thank you." A memory tries to surface and is pushed back down. "I think I remember someone else calling me that." I frown as I sit. "But I don't know who."

"Best to focus on the meal before you. We're going to have a full day." He sits as well and lays his napkin across his lap.

I mimic his actions as he slides four bacon strips and three round pancakes on a plate. "Here you go, my dear."

"Thank you, but you don't have to do that. I know how to fix a plate."

"I know you do, but I want to do this. For you." His eyes hold mine and he smiles at me.

"Well, thank you then." I accept the plate from his hand and sit it in front of me. I pour warm syrup all over the pancakes and start cutting them up. "You said 'we are going to have a full day' "? If no one is supposed to know I am here, how are we going to have a full day?"

He lays two bacon strips on his plate along with a pancake. "When my... friends leave, I shall need your consultation on a project I will be undertaking." This isn't him asking, but telling me what I would do.

"And what particular project do you think I have the skills for? We only just met yesterday. You don't know me, and I am just getting to know you." I start cutting up the rest of my food and begin eating.

He watches me as I start chewing. Satisfied I had

begun eating, he takes a bite himself. We eat in a strangely comfortable silence for several moments and then speaks.

"You love people and children. Your input on a renovation to my home will be paramount."

"You have a home?" I am sure he has slept there the night before, but wasn't sure how I know. "What sort of renovation are you looking for?"

"I have a need to add three new bedrooms to the home. Children's rooms. Nurseries." He takes another bite and I follow suit with him.

"Congratulations," I say, after I have swallowed the food in my mouth. "Will you be having more children, or grandchildren?"

He laughs out loud and lays down his fork. "Age is just a number, Judin. I am still old enough to father children. Why, I am only nine hundred and ninety-nine. My time may almost be at an end, but I can still sire children."

I gasp out loud. "Nine hundred and ninety-nine? Forgive me, but you can't be that old."

"Why? Do I look younger?" His right eyebrow shoots up and he laughs boisterously. "I am only kidding, my dear. Yes, I can still sire children, but do not wish to. It's almost another's turn, and I want him to be prepared." He cuts another bite of his pancake and takes the last bite of his food.

"Him?" I take another bite too, chewing, and swallowing it. "If you are as old as you say you are then who is this he? Your son?"

He watches me for a moment and then sits down his utensils carefully. "I'm going to Become someone new, my dear. And when I do, I would like you to welcome him with an open mind. I'll still be me, but better — newer." He leans back in his chair and looks out to the city below. "My youth will return and then maybe you will stop looking at me like a grandfather."

I blush. "I can't love you, if that is what you are inferring. My heart already belongs to someone else. Someone very near and dear to me."

His eyes harden. "And who might that be? I wish to know him."

I giggle out loud. "Whoever your chef is, good sir. He makes the best breakfast I have ever eaten." I finish my milk and orange juice, and stand. "If you will excuse me, I shall get ready for the day. Thank you for a lovely breakfast."

He stands too. A relieved expression on his face. "I will see you soon, my dear."

I turn and slip into the dressing room, shutting and locking the door behind me. I take my time dressing and getting ready for the day. I am not sure what Jaad is expecting me to do, so I want to be ready.

Upon emerging, the room is full of people again. No one pays attention to me as I move around the room to straighten the bed.

On a whim, I look up and see Jaad glance to me and then to the bed.

I stop working and sit down in the single overstuffed chair. I don't want to make the bed. Someone else will do it. I am sure of it.

Soon, the room is emptied of people except for Jaad and Christan. Jaad comes into the room and rests his hands behind his back. "May I?"

"Yes, I am ready." In my closet, I had only found stretch waist jeans and generous cut tops. There were a few dresses, but I am not a big fan. A wide brimmed straw hat with an ivory ribbon beckoned me to wear it. With all of the gold catching the heat from the suns, it has to be baking outside. But when I looked down earlier, no one seemed to mind.

Christan pushes a button and Jaad steps forward. He had changed into a light blue shirt and white cargo pants. Crisp white Vans rest on his feet. His eyes move up and down my body, as he offers me his arm. "You look lovely, my dear."

Christan opens a door and we step onto an elevator. I feel it ascending.

"Can women on this world become someone new too?" I ask, remembering our earlier conversation.

"Yes." His answer is curt.

The doors in front of us slide open and we are on the roof. A large multifaceted sphere looms over us. Sitting on the middle of the roof is a flying machine of some sort. I have never seen anything like it. It was as if someone took a helicopter and airplane and rethought the idea for each to make them one.

"It is automatically piloted. I've already set the course. Shall we?"

The blades are already turning on the machine, but it is quiet. He opens the door and I enter the cabin. It is one room, big enough for the two of us to walk around in comfortably. Jaad shuts the door behind us and starts walking to the back. I follow him.

"Should we sit while it takes off? Buckle up or something?"

Jaad opens a bottle of clear liquid and pours the liquid into two glasses. He hands one of them to me and sips the one in his other hand. "No need. As soon as the door close, we ascend. We should be at my home soon."

I lift my glass. "And this is?"

"All water for drinking is filtered and purified. There is a special ingredient added at the facility that maintains the city's water supply. That ingredient, when it is swallowed, compensates for the recipient's diet. In a fraction of a second, it reads what is needed and adds it their system. Nothing ever gets triggered by the person drinking it that is not necessary."

That is brilliant! "Sounds like a great way to help everyone."

"It is. My grandfather ran the testing in his lifetime and my father implemented it. Since then the health benefits have made a tremendous advantage to the people of this planet." He looks up and I follow his gaze. "We're here."

The door opens and I take a drink. Amazingly, it wasn't hot on the roof of the building we were on, but I'm not taking a chance that it will be the same outside the door.

"Thank you."

Jaad slides the glass from my hand and sits it down on a table. "Shall we?"

I walk out the door and he follows. We are parked outside the steps of a massive gold toned home. It is opulent and grand.

"This is lovely, but why didn't we walk here? It's a nice day out." It isn't massively hot like I thought it would be, it's comfortable. A good day to get out and enjoy the sunsshine.

"I'm glad you like the house, my dear." Jaad offers me his arm again. "I would like your opinion on a matter and, if you agreed, you could start on it more quickly if we flew instead of walked."

That made sense. Something is still off though.

"I wouldn't have minded the walk." I look up to the suns in the sky. How is the temperature not overbearingly hot?

He slides my arm through his and we begin walking. "How about we plan a walk for another day?"

Jaad is placating me. I am sure of it.

"Okay." It is nice being next to Jaad. Comforting.

Two huge doors open in front of us. A cozy open floor plan greets us. I love it immediately.

"It's brilliant!" I say, pushing myself closer to everything I can. The home is exceptionally beautiful.

"When you are done here, my dear, we will make our way to where the new addition shall be made." He patiently watches me oohing and ahhing over all that I lay my eyes upon.

"Oh, sorry. It's just... I think I love this home. You should be very proud." I turn to him, composing myself. My enthusiasm had gotten the best of me. "I'm ready now."

He chuckles again and begins taking me through the rest of the home. Up an elegant flight of stairs and through an open room, to a set of double doors that leads out onto a balcony. The view outside is green and lush.

"It's so pretty out here."

His hand pats mine, softly, and then he taps his ear. "Yes, it is. Close your eyes and tell me what you see. Remember, I need three children's nurseries: sizes, dimensions, everything. Don't hold back."

I close my eyes and see all of the rooms in vivid color. It is odd. It is as if I have seen them before and am seeing them again. I begin explaining it all to Jaad, as he stands beside me.

When I finish speaking, he nods his head. "So it shall be done."

I laugh. "There is no way you can remember all of that. I rattled it all off so fast." Subconsciously, I had moved closer to him as I spoke. I step back.

"I don't need to, my dear." He touches his ear again and this time I notice a small item inside it. "Everything has been noted as you are speaking. Designers, landscapers, , and anyone else needing to know can be working on the plans." He sighs, heavily. "I only hope I am still here when this section is completed."

"Oh, silly. You aren't going anywhere for quite a while. Now, what else can I do?"

We turn and begin our trek back to the flying machine.

"You're not done by a long way, my dear. There are plans to approve and changes to be made to make the additions you want. Oh, no. There will be long days and nights. Very little sleep and all that comes with this to complete this on time and correctly. We will draw up a schedule and itinerary when we return. And I bet you are getting hungry."

We had eaten a while ago, but I feel ravenous. "Yes, please."

"Lunch on the return and then work. Don't expect too much rest in the coming months. You have a job to perform." His laughter is like music.

"Yes, sir."

CHAPTER SIX
The Planning

*I*n the next couple of months, I throw myself into my work. Room design, color schemes, construction plans, and many more ideas are given to me as I had discussed them with Jaad. We have breakfast every morning and dine together almost every night. He is excellent company and I have come to admire him very much. It seems he is always working in his office.

I have had no other memory bubbles pop in my head over the last few months, as I fall into bed exhausted most nights.

Being almost stagnant within my body and not having a lot of room to move around is frustrating me more daily. My middle is rounding out and I want to at least maintain my weight.

I found an exercise room behind a door on the other side of my bed. I utilize that to its potential and have set a routine of working out. Being held in essentially a bedroom, with little room to move around, isn't good for me so I instigate a plan myself.

My closet doesn't accommodate my expanding girth. Another frustration. Couldn't it just size my clothes smaller, or I could insist Jaad let me out to walk. He could bring me smaller portions or healthier options. Lately, I want foods that I know aren't the best, but are comforting. If I have to be here, I want to be comforted. Sadly, food was my choice in bringing that comfort. Thus, the weight gain.

A desk appeared one afternoon after I awoke from a nap. When I moved to it, a screen appeared over it, allowing me to view the work being done on Jaad's home. It was exactly as I had envisioned.

Truth be told, I had almost forgotten about myself being a bird in a glass cage until one morning, as I was working, I happened to glance up and look over to Jaad. He was working alone at his tall desk, among computer screens, but it was what was behind him that captured my attention. On a ledge of the huge window was a blue bird. It wasn't just one shade of blue, but many. I was reminded of the sky blue of my home, the soft greys of rainy morning, and the sea as it churns during a storm. Elusive memories seductively brush my mind, but are held back by some unseen entity. I am not alone, even in my own head, and the thought becomes apparent during that moment. Someone else is with me, and that worried me a bit. The presence almost felt like a physical one, but that was impossible. Another person monitoring my thoughts was impossible too. I dismiss both ideas as I watch the bird flittering along the ledge. It moved, and chirped, but I couldn't hear it. As I looked beyond it, I saw the huge city that lies below. The bird was free to fly wherever it chose. It could move from place to place, going wherever it willed. While I am held an almost prisoner in a beautifully appointed cage. Where did my thought of escape go? Why did I suddenly envy a simple bird? When had I accepted my irons, and not the freedom I so desired?

I watched the bird until it spread its wings and flew away. I wanted to fly away too. I wanted to see what it sees, enjoy what it does, and be with it as it went wherever it chose.

Jaad left the room minutes before, off to some place he can go, and I cannot.

A tiredness overcomes me. I move to the bed. I take off my soft shoes and pull back the covers to lie down. I bring them up to my chin as I lie on my side.

I miss home. Earth is a memory; one I can access. My mother and father are there. I have no siblings to miss, but friends that will wonder where I am. Even my job as an Independent Contractor is a distant memory, one I only thought of as a time when I was me. Really me.

Except that isn't when I am really me. I am really me when... When....

Oh, blast! It is right there! The memories are right there, but I can't access them. Tears leak from my eyes. Liquid frustration pouring down my cheeks. Not because I miss Earth and all its enjoyment, but because I miss something else. Something I can't remember. Something vitally important to my existence. Something I want above all else.

How could I have forgotten it?

I wrap my arms around my thickening waist, as exhaustion pulls me under. A stabbing pain wracks my body, and I am wrenchied into a blackness. My eyes close and a memory begins.

***

I am lying in my bed, alone, and in the dark. We had gotten separate hotel rooms, as we always do when we travel. The light from the street softly illuminates the room, as I stare out the window, watching nothing.

He isn't in a good mood tonight, and I can't do anything to make him happy. There are times that he gets like this: all mercurial and inconsolable. I know nothing can comfort him, even myself. So, I bid him good night and go to my room.

I shouldn't cry over him, but I do. Too often. I shouldn't love him like I do, but I do. And maybe that was why I can't help hurting over him. I never want him to be unhappy, and he is. I know his mood will brighten by morning, but the waiting is the hardest part for me. If I didn't care, it wouldn't matter. But, God help me, I do, and I have no intention of stopping. He always cares for me, no matter where we go, yet never asks for anything in return. He never expects anything from me, but I give him everything. Every so often, I catch him watching me, then he glances away. It is as if he is waiting. For what, I don't know.

When he had transitioned from Thomael to Kinim, I didn't know what to expect. Kinim is entirely his own person: laughter, hugs, always touching, emotional, right, and willful. Thomael had been independent, angry, hardened, compassionate, caring, and always right. At least the two of them have that in common, even when they are wrong, they are right. I have learned to gently correct each, in such a way that it seems like they are the ones who were in control. Even when they aren't.

In the past five years I had travelled with Kinim through time and have seen many different places with him; no matter what, I had been put first. I couldn't help but do the same with him. There had been times of danger and intrigue, but there was also beauty and wonder. I have come to care for Kinim as much as I did Thomael. Maybe even more so, because I had started to care for Thomael just when he was leaving. Kinim took his place in my heart.

So, yes, laying here in bed, frustrated that I can't do a thing for him, is driving me crazy. I want to make everything right for him. But can't.

Or can I?

I slip on a robe and walk down to his hotel room door. As I knock, the door opens.

"Hey, Kinim, it's me, Judin." I shut the door behind me. "I knocked." I peer around the room.

He is sitting at the desk in a chair facing the door. His eyes glisten as the light hits them.

"Have you been crying? Are you alright?" I move to him and come to rest on my knees. "You were distant at dinner,

and I want to make sure you are okay." I look up at him. "Have you been crying?" I had never seen him cry, except for once. What caused those tears was a tragedy. We never speak of it.

He cocks his head to the side staring at me. His hand comes up and his fingertips lightly touch the side of my face.

I turn my head towards them, allowing myself to take a bit of happiness in his touch.

His hand drops to his lap. As he blinks, another silent tear falls.

"What happened? Will you talk to me?"

I feel the heaviness in his heart and it almost undoes me. I want to cry with him, over what, I don't know. But I find myself being sad with him.

"Why won't you talk to me?" I ask, face to face with him, staring into his eyes.

He isn't moving, but his nostrils flare.

I place my hand on his other lap. I bring up my arm and repeat the same action he had just performed on me.

His eyes close, as he leans into my touch. He revels in it. I repeat the motion.

"Is that what you need? Do you need to be touched?"

His chest moves in and out, his breath is loud. Another tear.

I bring my other hand to his face and stroke both sides at once. His face is visibly relaxing. I do it again, and he lays his back.

I do it again and his hands move to the arms of the chair. I was getting a response.

After a fourth sweep of my fingertips, his head moves slowly. His eyes open, the irises turning black. In the dark it almost looks like both of his eyes have gone pitch black. But it must be a trick of the light.

"What are you doing to me, min eurozan?" His voice low and throaty.

It has been a long time since he had called me 'min eurozan'.

"I want to bring you peace and show you that I care for you." I sweep my fingertips down the sides of him again, enjoying the feel of his light stubble. "You aren't alone, Kinim. I'll always be with you."

"Am I your heart?" The words he says bespeaks a vulnerability and trust.

"You have always been my heart. My Everything. All that I am is yours." I reply, repeating the action again.

His hands grip the chair tightly, and the wood creaked.

"Say it. Say I am min eurozan, your heart."

If he needs to hear me say the words to him, then I will. I will always give him whatever he needs.

Leaning forward I move closer to his ear. His scent wraps around my senses and pulls me closer. I lick my lips and take a deep breath, drawing him into myself, and then speak. "Min eurozan."

His hands shoot off of the chair and cup my upper arms, securing him to me. He scoots forward and comes close to my ear. I hear his breath, feel its warmth, and shiver. "Lie with me."

"Yes." I agree, readily. I have wanted him, since I knew I loved him.

He turns and takes another deep breath through his nose. There is no exhalation. "Say you will do whatever I ask."

"Yes." I shiver from the heat I feel radiating from his body. Soon, I will feel that on my flesh.

Kinim rises from his seat and takes my hand, bringing me up with him. He turns me in his arms, my back to his front. They come around me and I place my hands on his.

I feel his head bob up and down once. From the shadows emerges a man from my past. One I thought I would never see again.

"Thomael?" I glance behind me to Kinim and back to Thomael. "But how?"

"In your timeline, I have been Kinim for five years. In this moment, in my timeline, I am still me."

I am torn between wanting to run to Thomael and stay in Kinim's arms. Tears spring from my eyes. "I have missed you."

Thomael glances to Kinim and then to me. "No hug for me then?"

"Go to him, Judin. He loves you too." Kinim urges, but I need no further words from him.

I launch myself from Kinim and run straight into Thomael's arms. They close around me, and I feel like I am home. Thomael is back, and I don't care why or for how long. I can hold him, at least for a while.

"You always have every part of me."

His hand comes to my head and begins massaging my scalp. "Is that a promise, min eurozan?"

My toes curl, as I to enjoy the feel of Thomael's hands. My senses are pushed into overdrive, as everything comes at me. "Always."

Another body presses behind me. Kinim.

I bring one of my arms from Thomael, palming Kinim's face. He leans into my hand.

"We shall have you then." Kinim wraps his arm around my waist and pulls against his front.

Thomael moves with us, and I am in the middle of them.

Kinim's lips find the pulse point in my neck, while Thomael begins exploring my body with his hands. I turn my head to kiss Kinim, while Thomael peels the robe from me.

I have never been intimate with two men. One man, yes, but not two. aren't Thomael and Kinim technically the same person?

I stand between them as they treasure me. My mind derails as they begin lavishing my entire body with caresses and kisses. Kinim draws us toward the bed, not breaking contact as we make our way.

The time comes and I know I am ready for them. Kinim moves to sit with his back to headboard and my back to his front.

Thomael moves into position and takes me, not finishing

himself, but moving so that Kinim can have his turn. Both men are gentle and loving. I never thought any time like this would happen, or be as tender.

Kinim takes his time loving me, as Thomael holds me in his arms. Healso refrains from finishing.

Instead, he looks to his right and moves to my left. Standing beside us is a man with red hair. His look to me is filled with love.

Curious at who this new man may be, I turn my head to Kinim. "This is Jerren, min eurozan. You'll meet him very soon. He is one of us. Jerren thinks of you as his eurozan."

I glance back to Jerren, not taking the time to wonder what he thinks of me having two men already in the bed. But, if this will be one of Kinim's next selves, he wouldn't mind. Would he?

Thomael and Kinim are mine. I have already accepted that fact. Allowing Jerren to have a part of me will be easy. All three men are One. To love one means loving all three.

"You have not met him yet, but you will." He pauses, and then continues to speak, near my ear. His voice is low and seductive. "When I am gone. He wants to love you too. Will you share yourself with him? He wants you as much as we do."

Of course he does. They are all One. Thomael loves me, as does Kinim. Jerren will want me too.

I stop caressing the back of Thomael's neck with my hand and bring it out to Jerren. "Min eurozan." I breathe out a sigh, waiting for my love.

He sheds his clothes and joins me on the bed.

Kinim lays on my right side and Jerren on my left. Thomael grasps my ankles as his eyes find the center of my body. He licks his lips as I feel him enter me slowly. Becoming one, he stops and closes his eyes. His hands grasp my hips, bringing me closer to him. His eyes open and the light blue has turned to the color of the sky during an angry storm. I swear I see flashes of lightning in them.

He looks to Kinim and to Jerren then his eyes find mine. I feel their eyes on me and hear three voices in unison. "Min eurozan."

Thomael's loving is hard and powerful. He doesn't just want to use my body, but brand me as his. He wants my perfect submission, so I give him everything.

His time comes too soon and he exhausts himself. I vaguely hear Kinim and Jerren's breath catch, as Thomael lies down on the bed.

Thomael slides to my side, as Jerren sits behind me, bringing me close.

Kinim has his way with my body, enterings me swiftly, while kissing my neck and face. As Kinim's moment comes, his dark eyes stare into my soul.

I hear Jerren hiss between his teeth. It is as if he is experiencing the other man's feelings. I marvel how both men love so differently, yet the same.

Kinim moves from me and fluffs all of the pillows, laying them behind me.

Jerren tentatively kisses me, as he has his way with me. His eyes never leaves mine the entire time we love one another. As his time comes, he briefly closes his sage green eyes, releasing himself.

He slides to my left side, as Kinim comes up on my right. Thomael lays his head on my stomach, breathing us in. I wrap my arms around Kinim and Jerren, bringing them close. Both men bring one of their hands to my chest and their breathing evens out.

Thomael is the last to succumb to sleep. As he does, I hear him whisper. "Min eurozan."

All three men are now asleep, while I cradle them close to me. This moment is sheer perfection. This is a time I want to happen again and again. If we can be like this for the rest of eternity, I would be content.

In this room, the four of us are happy and there is peace. They have declared their love for me, and I for them. Nothing *would ever change how we feel about one another.*

***

"Judin?"

I feel a hand on my face, but don't want to wake up. I am dreaming of three men who love me and I love them. The stabbing pain in my body has lessened, in light of the lovemaking.

"Judin? Wake up, my dear."

I fight the compulsion, pushing against my brain. It is wanting what I don't – to become conscious. I want to stay here with Kinim, Jerren, and Thomael.

"Min eurozan." I whisper, as I reach up, eyes still closed, to lightly graze Jaad's face with my fingertips. "I love you. I love you all."

I bring myself up and touch my lips to Jaad's. His gasp is audible.

"You are one. They are you." I bring my arms around his neck and pull him close. I open my eyes and stare straight into his. "Thomael. Kinim. Jaad. Jerren. It doesn't matter what name you call yourself, you are still mine and I am still yours."

One of his arms snake behind my back and draws me close. The other hand lifts to my face, grazing it with his fingertips.

"I did not think you would recognize me, min eurozan. It has been so long since last we met."

My eyes find his. I want to erase the lines from the face I love, say something that would bring him peace and joy. "I would recognize my love anywhere." I lean up to kiss him again.

As our lips part, he frowns down at me. "I had to wait my entire lifetime for you to find me. I am yours and you are mine. I have known this day was coming and anticipated it with every passing hour." He frowns, sadly. "I am about to Become, min eurozan. I've lived many years, waiting for you to be brought to me."

"I'm here now." With one hand I reach down to push the covers off of me. My body is ready for his. "Lie with me."

His snow white head shakes back and forth. "Time has been too long, and I must go. I came to tell you that when you next see me, I will be someone else. Someone who loves you very much."

"You can't leave me." Even as I say it, I know they aren't true. He has to leave me. Thomael did, and when he returned, I loved him still. "But you must. I will wait for your return."

His fingertips stroke my cheek and I savor his touch. The light returns to his hazel eyes. "I have, and always will, love you. I yours. Forever."

He presses his lips to mine and then withdraws from me.

"But how will I know you?" I ask, as he moves to other side of the room. "I need to know how to know you." I sit up, pulling the covers to me.

"Your soul will know," he replies, turning from me to open the same door that had taken us to the elevator leading to his flying machine.

"Jaad?" I call, running from the bed to him.

He catches me in his arms and pulls me close. I bring a hand to his hair and another behind his back. We had four comfortable months to get to know one another and now our time is gone. It is too soon, and he doesn't know. I have never told him.

"I love you, min eurozan. I'll always love you." I pull him down for another kiss. This one is long and deep. I'm trying to tell him so many things with my touch.

"I love you too, min eurozan," he repeats, and then slowly lets me go. "Wait for me," he says and then shuts the door behind himself.

"Forever," I say to the closed door and lean against it, willing myself not to cry.

CHAPTER SEVEN
The Visitation

*F*our weeks later, I awake with the suns streaming through the window. I don't want to open my eyes. If I do, I know Jaad won't be there.

You can do this, I say to myself, hoping I can believe it.

I choose to be brave and push back the covers. I put my feet on the floor and stand, cautiously. No matter how much exercising and cutting back on what I ate, I continued to gain weight. My stomach is beginning to round out. I am hungry all the time, too. That doesn't help me, as I try to keep myself in some sort of shape.

The office is quiet. It's so new, as I am used to hearing Jaad talking and moving around at all hours. I make my way to the bathroom and use it, taking the time to wash up afterwards. When I look up in the mirror, I see myself. I look older than I was five months ago.

Had it really been five months? Where had I started out? From Earth?

"On a journey," I hear myself say. Except it's not me. It's a boy, and he's very young by the sound of his voice.

"We can hear your thoughts." A second male voice speaks, sweetly.

I hear them both clearly, as if they are standing beside

me. I turn in a circle, but don't see anyone.

"Who said that?" I ask, looking for cameras or recording equipment. "Who's talking?"

"We are." Three voices chime in simultaneously in my mind.

I look around again, but don't see anyone.

"I'm going crazy." After all these months, I've finally snapped.

A giggle and then the first boy speaks again. "Look down."

I do, but see nothing.

"Inside." The first boy, says in an authoritative tone.

I place a hand just below my rounding. Am I pregnant?

"Yes." All three voices answer together again, each with their distinctive personalities.

How? When? Why don't I remember being with their father?

"We are theirs." The third voice explains, tenderly.

Theirs?

The past rushes at me as I grab onto the bed, holding on tightly. Every memory that has been suppressed resituates itself in my brain.

I remember everything!

Thomael. Kinim. Jerren. Am I carrying the products of our loves?

"Yes." The second male voice replies, patiently.

"How old are you all?" I ask, my palm over where I know they now lay.

"Five months," the first voice replies, knowingly. "I am Thomael's son."

"And I am Kinim's son," speaks the second son.

"I am Jerren's," says the third son, out loud.

All of these voices are in my head, but I hear them as if they are outside of me.

Thomael's son speaks again. "You don't have to talk out loud to hear us. We have heard your thoughts since we were conceived. We know our fathers and who they are. You are their min eurozan, and we all love you too."

"Indubitably." Kinim's son, agrees.

"Absolutely." Jerren's son, intonates.

I move to the closet and notice all of the clothes are now bigger. Maternity wear. It has changed to meet my needs. I walk to the mirrored desk with a thickly padded bench in front of it and sit. "Your fathers are gone, little ones." I sniffle. "They had to go and I'm afraid you will never see them."

"Nope." Thomael's son says in the same hang-the-rules fashion his father used. "Time isn't linear, mother. We can see our dad's any time we want after we are born."

"Without a doubt." Jerren's son says.

"I can't wait to see my father. I bet he is brilliant." Kinim's son, excitedly says. "He has to be, he's my dad!"

I had never thought about it that way. The three of us had jumped through time and space together. Of course we could see their fathers, any time we want. Yes, as soon as I can, I will make that happen.

"It's a plan, boys." I spring up, selecting the clothes I would dress in for the day. I take my time now, knowing I am carrying three little lives inside of me.

"You miss him. Jaad." Kinim's son says, sadly. "Even though he said he would be back for you."

"He took a part of me with him," I reply out loud, as I begin to brush my hair. "He didn't even tell me who he was. Not that he was..." Who is Jaad to my sons? Their dad, stepdad, great grandfather?

"How do I remember all of your fathers and the time I spent with them?" I have spent months not remembering anything and suddenly there it all is. "Why now?"

"Because it's time." Kinim's voice comes to me now. It isn't my imagination, but from behind me.

I look into the mirror and there he stands. The soft grey of his shirt begging me to touch it. His tanned face asking for my fingertips. A smile as radiant as the suns.

"Kinim," I said, lovingly. "Min eurozan."

"Min eurozan." He repeats, softly. "Hello." One of his hands lightly falls on my shoulders.

I reach up and lay one of my hands on his. I have missed his touch. "When did you get here?"

"A while ago. We were watching you while you were speaking to our sons." He squeezes my shoulder, reassuringly. "You are going to make an excellent mother."

"We?" I peer around him and see Thomael. "Thomael? How? When?" I stand and make my way over to him.

He welcomes me with open arms. "Min eurozan."

"I missed you, too." I say, bringing my arms around him. When I look up, he captures his lips with mine.

As he pulls from me, I glance around us. "Where is Jerren? Why is he not here?"

Kinim moves up to us and wraps his arms around my waist, pulling me toward him. Thomael follows us. "Jerren will be along soon."

"Don't you want to spend time with us?" Thomael teases.

Kinim drops his hands to where our sons lay. "We have missed you very much." His head lands softly on my shoulder. He brings himself flush with my body.

Thomael follows suit. I am between two of the men I love.

"It seems like ages since I have seen you both." I bring a hand up and around Kinim's neck. My other hand wraps around Thomael's waist. His hands rest on my hips, possessively. "Jerren is another piece of my heart." I bring my hand from Thomael's waist to the back of his head. "You are all pieces of my heart."

One of Kinim's hands splay lightly around my neck, turning it carefully to him. His gaze falls to my lips, as he wets his own with his tongue. "Kiss me."

I can't resist such a decadent request. As my head leans back, Kinim captures my mouth with his, coaxing it open. Of course I love them both, with no preference. But for some reason, I always welcome Kinim's touch more than the others. I liken it to a constant craving.

As he moves from my lips, Thomael rests a hand on the nape of my neck. "But it is my Will you wish to pursue, isn't it?"

"Yes, min eurozan," I acquiesce.

He isn't leaning forward to kiss me, like I thought he would, but drops to his knees. Kinim moves his hands from over the children to my hips, cradling them.

Thomael leans forward and places his forehead gently where Kinim's hands had been. "My son. I hear you speaking to your mother, and to myself. Very soon I will hold you in my arms and I will rejoice in that day." He moves forward and lifts my shirt. His warm breath moving across my skin. Thomael reverently kisses the spot where our sons lay. "I love you, min filjo."

His eyes close, as he begins weeping silently. I bring a hand to his head, stroking his short, spiky hair.

"He loves his son, min eurozan. In time, he will come to love all of our sons. They are all him in a different lifetime."

I look to Kinim with a smile. "And you? Do you love just your son, or all of our boys?"

His smile brightens my world. "They are, in a way, me. I get to love them all. Especially because you are their mother. You nurture them with your body and with your love."

Right answer, I think, reaching back to him for another kiss. His lips meet mine again, briefly, as he pulls his head back from me. "We can't stay long, min eurozan. Jaad found us and suggested that we visit you now. That, at this moment, he is Becoming. His thought, even as he is transitioning, is for you and our sons."

Thomael turns his head toward us. "I can see why you love us." He rests his head over oursons again.

"We love you very much, min eurozan." Kinim recites, lovingly.

Thomael stands and carefully lays the fabric of my shirt flat again. "We must go." His eyes change to a turbulent blue. "But we will have you again soon."

"'See'." Kinim interjects, eyeing Thomael. "We will see you again soon."

Thomael leans down, kissing me soundly on the lips. "No, I mean have. She's delicious and I plan to drink from her soon."

Drink? As in? I place a hand over my mouth.

Thomael's hand comes out and he points an index finger at me. "Exactly."

Kinim shakes his head and then nods. "You are right. We were much too hasty with her last time." He looks down to me. In his eyes is a promise. "Next time, we feast."

I clear my throat, trying not to show my anticipation.

Kinim's lips fit over mine, as he takes his time kissing me.

"Tick tock, K." Thomael glances at the door and then back to us.

Kinim lifts his lips from mine and flashes Thomael a look. "You know I hate being called, K." Another quick peck and he is at the door with Thomael. "We shall see you soon, min eurozan."

"I shall look for you both always," I answer, bringing my hands over my slightly swollen middle. "Shan't we boys?"

"Yes, momma." Three male voices chant. They have been suspiciously quiet while their fathers were here.

Thomael marches out the door, ready for his next adventure.

"Kinim?"

He is all ready to walk out the door too, but turns when I said his name. "Yes, min eurozan?"

"Did you get a chance to talk," I lift a hand and gesture to my middle, "to your son?"

"When I wasn't speaking to you, I was talking to him. He's a lot like his father. We will all get along very well." He pivots on one foot and marches out the door. No good-bye.

He hated good-byes.

"I guess it's just the four of us, until your father gets home."

Their father. I am back to that. Will the next man who Jaad is, be their father? Will they know him as dad? How will they address him?

"He's our father too, mom. They are all him. So, we shall call him father as well."

It is all confusing to me. On that note, I decide to let them all figure it out.

I need to dress for the day now. The next Thomael or Kinim or Jaad will come through the door, and I will need to be ready for him. I know I will always be ready for him. This time my a will know him, and I will welcome him with open arms.

CHAPTER EIGHT
The Waiting

I think every day I will see him, my next min eurozan, as I work on the room additions for Jaac's children – our children. Every time the door opens or someone new comes through the door, I hope it will be him.

But he has yet to materialize.

Hours became days, days bled into weeks. Weeks miraculously turned into months. Before I know it, I am well rounded, with three new lives thriving inside of me.

Shortly after Thomael and Kinim came to visit, Christan welcomed a new person into our small circle. It is Janele, the woman who first found me when I arrived. She is Elorcui's idea of a doctor or healer. Her treatment is far beyond anything I have ever heard any of my pregnant female friends speak of. I am being monitored once a week and hear the children's heart rates. My meals and exercise habits are adjusted to meet our changing needs. Everything I do, especially now, as close as I am to giving birth, is for the children.

Even my closet has changed to meet my requirements. All of my clothes have become maternity or loose fitting. I have no more heels or low heels, but cushioned shoes that hug my feet. Everything I need to feel comfortable, miraculously appeared, ready to be utilized.

The only thing missing from my life are the men who helped father these children.

Father? They are all the same man, so it would be father. Right?

I crumple and toss the paper I am working on to the floor of the room and glance to the monitor on my desk. It shows in real time the goings on at Jaad's home. If Jaad was the result of a Becoming, then where is the next one? My new min eurozan?

"Stupid bloody work." I sit down in the oversized chair in my room, wishing I had someone to rub my feet and back. Both have been hurting a lot lately and it would be heaven to have someone to minister to them.

Christan approaches my room. "Judin?"

"Enter."

He pushes the button on the wall and makes his way over to me. I forgotten that I had told him to put up the invisible partition.

"What is it?" I am short tempered, and he knows it. Let him try carrying three children in his womb! "I'm sorry." I say, lumbering to my feet. "Is there something I can do for you, Christan?"

"I was wondering if there is anything I can do for you?" He stands at attention so stiffly that I think he may break in a good wind.

"Relax." I throw up my hands. "You stand straight all day long with a blank expression on your face." I step forward. "What do you think about, behind that mask you wear?"

"Honestly, my family." He exhales, and relaxes his stance a little. "I miss them daily and can't wait to get home to them at night."

I sit down in one of the chairs in the room.

Christan pushes a button at the door, locking it from the inside. Anyone wanting in, will need to communicate before entering.

"Sit down. The door is locked. Take a load off."

"If it's all the same to you." He goes back to stand by the door.

"Whatever. What time does Janele come by today?" I rest my hands, on my enormously rounded stomach and watch him.

He stares straight ahead, as his eyes find mine again. "In about forty-five minutes."

"Where did you go? Just then. It is like you were gone for a moment and then came back."

"Eidetic memory. Everyone on the planet has one. We memorize everything and never forget all that we have seen. Combine that with an internal harmony of time and there is nothing we don't know."

"Doesn't that get boring? Always knowing everything?" I ask, beginning to stand carefully.

Christan moves forward, but I wave him away.

The children are talking to one another, and occasionally, they let me in on their conversations. As I get bigger, they complain about space in which to move. I can't do anything about it, but suggest they place nicely together until they are born.

In truth, it is slightly distracting, but I don't mind. I love them, and want to hear their voices.

"Not really. It's nice to know what to expect. Although, there are always fluctuations in frequencies that cause unknown occurrences."

"A surprise." I ponder, out loud. "If I have what you do, I would love it."

"If you grew up with an eidetic memory and in tune with the universe," he says, turning his head slightly to the side, "it becomes a part of who you are. If not, then it is unfamiliar. Possibly even unsafe."

"Very true." I move to look out the window. My only view of the life below. A world I never truly, in my almost thirty-five weeks of being here, never got to explore. "Have you heard anything? From him?"

"No. I know that some Becomings are easier than others. Often a Becoming takes time. Maybe his is one of them." He shrugs his shoulders, glancing out the window, then back to me. "He will come back to you."

"And if he doesn't?" I turn to him now, and bring my hands behind my back. It hurts to do, so I stop and bring them over my round belly. "What shall I do then, Christan? I've been a bird in a gilded cage. What do I do if he doesn't comeback?"

"Pardon me, but you already know what to do. You live." He gestures to the room. "Even I don't know everything, but I do know, without a doubt, that in that room is where he will find you." He swings his gaze back to me. "Don't give up hope."

I peek at him. "Can I go outside?"

He frowns, sadly.

"I miss the sun on my face and the grass beneath my feet." I hold out my hands. "I miss people." I drop a hand and push it out. "No offense, but I have seen people moving down there. Day by day, living their lives, eating the food. I want to be one of them."

"I've been instructed to wait until your Mate returns." Christan says, quietly. He's only following orders, but doing so reluctantly.

"Fine." I say, making my way to the bedroom. "My back and feet hurt anyway. I think I will soak in the tub. If I'm not out before Janele gets here, please tell her where I am."

"I shall." Christan presses the button, blocking me from view. I still see him, but he is staring straight ahead again. I hope he is thinking of his family, of his happy times with them.

And I pray I will have memories like that of my own, with my sons and their father.

In the bath, I undress and start running the warm water. I don't add any scents or perfumes. I lower myself into the tub, waiting for the heat to unknot my muscles and ease the strain of my body.

I lean my head back on the soft plastic pillow and close my eyes.

"Mom!" Thomael's son. Of course it is.

"Yes, dear," I answer him in my mind. I have given up speaking to them out loud.

"He won't move his foot and it's in my eye."

Ouch! "He who? There are two other boys in there with you."

"Jerren's son. He says his foot is comfortable... in my eye!" He yells and I flinch.

"Boys. Boys. You're both pretty." I hear Kinim's son laugh at that. "If at all possible, please remove your foot from your brother's eye."

"But momma," Jerren's son begins.

"No, but momma. Please try to do as I say so."

"Alright."

I feel a shift in the middle of my body as the boys move.

"Mommy!" Kinim's son. Oh, boy, I think, here he goes. "Thomael's son just hit me on the knee with his elbow."

"Alright guys, enough is enough! Play nicely or I swear I will find a way to come in there and jerk a knot in all three of your tails." I say, having enough of it.

"Okay."

"Alright, momma."

"Sorry, mommy."

Would I be forever breaking up fights between my sons? Oy vey!

There is a knock on my door, as I feel something loosen from inside of me. It is like a plug has been pulled, and with it, a great tearing and pain.

I scream loudly, and the door is opened. Janele steps inside and I see a ribbon of blood start to seep from the middle of my body.

"Out of the tub. Now."

I go to stand but I feel gravity pulling me back down again. "I can't." When did I become such a whiner? I push myself to my feet and I hear a splash in the tub. A great amount of yellow fluid lays in a puddle below me.

"You're very lucky I am the one of the few doctors who do an abundant amount of homework." She takes my elbow and helps me out of the tub.

"Why is that?"

"Because," she says, as we walk gingerly from the bath to the bedroom, "I've not seen a pregnancy like this in over a thousand years."

I stop in my tracks. The pain is pure torture, and now my confidence is shaken. "What?" My mind reels. "Then how?"

My body is still leaking fluid and a tiny ribbons of blood now, but she releases me to pull in a big round chair with a large hole in the bottom.

She walks back over and takes my elbow again. "Your men should be here any time now. No matter where they are, biology knows, and it will call them to you."

"Biology? Calling?" Across space and time? Is that possible? I was beginning to believe anything is possible with them.

"Yes, Judin. The father and mother are always present at the birth. The father is the one who will deliver the child. As you have three, I am sure they all will be here presently." There is no judgement in her voice but all facts.

"Their fathers will deliver them? You mean?" I attempt leaning down, it spreads my pelvis and I feel the urge to bear down.

"Yes."

Oh, lovely. They aren't here for months and then, at the final presentation, they show up?! Seriously? Is this how all relationships went on Elorcui? Because if it is, I am out before I am even in.

"You have... extenuating circumstances," she says, coming over to help me upright. "Please allow me to help you sit down."

She helps me onto the big doughnut and encourages

me to spread my legs open. I'm naked and slippery. Lucky for me, at the ends of the arms of the chair are handles. I place my hands in them and feel it begin to massage my hands. The back of the chair starts a massaging motion too and I feel warmth where I am sitting.

She takes a small tube from the bag, that she always brings, spreading something on her hands and arms.

"This is to sterilize me, so I can see how ready you are to birth your sons."

Janele sits on her knees and reaches for me. As she moves her hand, she talks. "I had my Mate find this birthing chair for you. I've cleaned and sterilized it. The bed will service as a place for them to be checked over, once the fathers and you have Bonded with them."

Her hand is bloody, as she takes it from me. I swear she probably felt my tonsils, as far as she stuck her hand up into me. "You are the perfect size to have them. No ripping on the outside. Everything looks fine. I can administer something for your pain, if you like."

I'm in an excruciating pain, but welcome it. "Not now. Thank you."

There is a knock at the door and then another.

"It looks like your Mates are here." She nods her head at me. "Christan, please answer the door."

He does and I see Thomael and Kinim move swiftly through it.

"She's here," Thomael says, his nostrils flaring. His head turns to us and then to Christan.

Janele covers me carefully with a fresh towel from the bath.

"I need to see her." Kinim's head swivels my way and I see his nostrils flare too.

Are they Scenting me out?

They can't see me, but I can see them. They are looking everywhere around the area I am in. I can sense their frustration building. Thomael looks ready to break down a wall. Dark clouds gather over Kinim's face. He can be the most unforgiving when he is unjustly wronged. I've seen it.

Janele runs to grabs two more towels from the bath and comes back to the room. "Let them in."

CHAPTER NINE
The Arrivals

*a*s soon as Christan pushes the button, he exits the room. Kinim locks the door behind him and Thomael rushes to me.

"Who are you?" He eyes Janele. "What's happening?" He moves to his knees and tries to peer under the warm towel. "It's time. I heard his call from across space and time. What do I do?"

"I'm Janele. I've been monitoring your Mate since she arrived here. Everything is well and the little ones are healthy. It's time for them to be born." Janele takes out the tube and hands it to Thomael as another pain rips through me.

Kinim walks over to us and comes to his knees too. "What do you want us to do for her? For our sons?"

Thomael hands the tube to Kinim.

"We haven't birthed a child, let alone three of them, in a while now," she says, nervously. "Each of you, squeeze a bit out of the tube. It's for sterilization. You are going to deliver your sons."

Thomael and Kinim do as instructed and pass the tube back to Janele, who stores it away.

"We get to deliver them?" A wide smile crosses Kinim's face as he elbows Thomael. "Do you hear that? We get to hold our sons."

Thomael looks sick. "I didn't know that is expected of us."

Seriously, I think, sitting up in the birthing chair and glaring at Thomael. I reach out a hand and grab a handful of the medium blue sweatshirt he always insists on wearing. "You were man enough to put your son in me, mister, you are going to be man enough to take him out. Do you hear me?"

Kinim chuckles at Thomael's horrified expression.

Letting go of his sweatshirt, I lean carefully into the rigid arms of the birthing chair.

Janele stands and makes her way through the closet door, still open from her previous trips. "I'll wash up and check you again."

She is back in a flash, reapplies the lotion, and does a final check. "You are ready to deliver. Take your time. Nice and easy now. They can wait on you."

I can feel the boys shifting in my body, each eager to make an appearance, and not wanting to wait on the other.

"Me first." Jerren's son.

"No, me." Thomael's son.

"If we are going to do this chronologically, then I believe I am second. But being as mommy loves me more, I should be first... or last, so I can be admired more. The last one always get the most attention."

I sigh loudly, inwardly.

"Boys. Boys. You will each get your turn."

Thomael's son shifts into position and begins his descent. "Here I go."

His father is already there, ready to catch him. I begin pushing as Janele suggested, but I have never seen Thomael more nervous. He keeps on changing the positions of his hands, so Janele tells him how to hold them. Now that she is instructing him, he holds them still.

I continue the process of pushing Thomael's son from me.

Thomael sees the crown of his son's head, he starts crying. "There he is!"

"Yes, yes. Now, when you are ready push him from you, Judin."

I watch Thomael as he glances from me to his son. "Please, min eurozan, show me my son."

After a few more pushes, his son emergesfrom my body and ready for Thomael to receive him. He pulls our son close and nestles him in his arms as if he is made to be there. "My son," he says, out loud, and then begins speaking to him in his mind. I can hear them speaking words of love and promises of tomorrows to come. "I name you, Lanon. Welcome to Elorcui, Lanon, min filjo."

He turns Lanon towards me and slips him into my arms. "Hello, Lanon, min filjo." I look to his father. "He's perfect."

"Mommy?" Kinim's son grabs my attention now.

I pass Lanon to Thomael. "Someone else is ready to be born." He stands with our son in his arms and begins walking around the room. Although he is silent, I can still hear him speaking to Lanon.

"Min eurozan." Kinim touches my face with his fingertips. "I have thought about you every moment of every hour of every day. You are, and have, every part of me. You always will."

"I love you, Kinim."

"And I love you, Judin." He looks down to where he will meet his son. "When you are ready."

"I am ready, mommy." His son says, eagerness in his voice.

"I know you are, son," I answer in my mind.

Bearing down twice and he crowns. Light and tears glisten in Kinim's eyes. I get to give him a son! Pushing a couple more times, he exits my body and sliding into Kinim's arms. Kinim pulls him close and nestles his son. "Welcomes to Elorcui." He glances to me. "What should we name him?"

Unlike Thomael, Kinim is allowing me to help choose a

name. "I like Josiah."

"And I like Steve." He thinks for a moment and then glances back to me. "How about Joeve?"

I nod my head.

"Hello, nuetre filjo." Kinim looks to me. I tilt my head to catch his gaze, as he speaks. "Nuetre meaning, our."

"Our son." I like that Kinim acknowledges Joeve as ours and not just his. Although I don't doubt that if anyone questions Thomael, he will answer that I am Lanon's mother.

Kinim lays Joeve in my arms. He's a perfect fit and my heart rejoices in his touch. I knew I loved him when he was still in my womb. Now that he is out, my love increases.

"Momma? Is it my turn?" Jerren's son is ready to make his entrance, but his father hasn't arrived.

"Jerren's son is ready to be born, Kinim, but he's not here."

I look to Janele. Her look is one of helpless concern.

"Where is Jerren?" Kinim glances behind him to Thomael. "Every atom was pulling me to this one place in time. Was it the same for you?"

"Yes." He glances swiftly to Kinim and back to our son. "I had to leave everything to be here for Judin and Lanon. Like you, I felt a pull to be right here, right now."

I bring my eyes back to Kinim. "You will be Jerren, Kinim. Can you be here while I deliver his son?"

He turns to glance at Janele. "Is that possible? Can I deliver another Becoming's son?"

He will do it! I am so relieved!

"In theory, if the father can't be available for the birth, another can do it." She hesitates then continues. "But Jerren's child is tied to his Becoming. His son will know you as his father, and never Jerren. If he should return."

I have no doubts that, if Kinim has to, he will claim Jerren's son as his. "Like imprinting?"

"Yes." Janele agrees. "But if they meet he will know Jerren as his father, but not like Kinim will be. The decision has to be made carefully."

Kinim's gaze rests on me. "The longer we wait, the more we put Jerren's and your child in danger, Judin. It's your call." He is still holding Joeve as he speaks. "Joeve and Jerren's son will become more than brothers, closer than they would be if Jerren was here."

Jerren! I want him here! I want him to catch his son when he exits me! I want so much I can't have. Because Jerren isn't coming through the door.

Maybe he isn't ever coming? I want my son to know the joys of having a father. Kinim will make the perfect dad for him.

One last glance at the closed, quiet door, and I know my answer. "Hand Joeve to Janele. You will catch Jerren's son."

Kinim stands and gives Joeve to Janele. His gaze hardens on the woman. "That is a piece of my heart. Treat him with care."

I shiver at what would befall anyone who committed a wrong to Kinim or his son. He could be the most unforgiving of the Becomings.

"Are you alright?" He bends down, holding out his arms, as he had done for Joeve. "Is he ready? I can't hear him speaking to you. Not like you can."

"Yes." I grasp the handles and stare longingly at the door. Come on, Jerren!

"Then push. You will have another son, and," he pauses, "so will I."

I bear down once and stop to breathe. Another breath and Jerren's son crowns outside of me.

"Daddy?" Jerren's son asks in my mind.

"Your father loves you very much, son." I answer him, not saying that his father isn't here for his birth. Something terrible must have happened to him. A piece of my soul begins bleeding for my lost love.

But I don't have time to dwell. The need to bear down is too great!

Suddenly, there is frantic knocking at the door. I can't stop delivering Jerren's child. He is already on his way out of my body.

Thomael unlocks the door and it swings open.

Jerren tears into the room, frantic. "My son. My Mate. They need me."

Kinim stands and takes Joeve from Janele. Janele retrieves the tube and squirts some on Jerren's hands. "Rub them together quickly."

He does so and holds out his arms just in time to catch his son.

"Jerren!" I pant, ecstatic that my love has made an appearance. "You came!"

He only has eyes for his son. "Of course I came, min eurozan. The Becoming was harder than I had ever experienced, but I made it through for you," his eyes find mine, "and our son. I had to find my way to you both. Every molecule in my body was pulling me here."

Kinim and Thomael exchange looks.

I glance to Janele. "The pair Bondings are strong, Judin. This is a good thing, for you and for your sons. It will keep their fathers close to them, and to you."

"Yeah." I watch all three of the men, smiling down to their sons. Close, like they had been for the last nine months. Their presence almost non-existent.

Thomael and Kinim exchange unhappy glances.

A thought occurs to me. "Jerren. You are him, aren't you? You are Jaad?"

His green eyes catch and hold mine. "Yes. I was here for the first four months of you carrying our sons."

Our sons.

I glance to Kinim who is watching me now. A handsome smile graces his features. He nods his head once and then turns back to our son.

"But you were old?" I still maintain eye contact.

"And time is all twisty. We are not subject to time. It is

subject to us." He frowns at me and then smiles to our son. "I'm sorry I couldn't be here sooner."

I bring my hand to his. "But you are here now. And that is what matters, min eurozan."

"What shall we name him, my dear? Something grand, like our love."

"Leeiss." I don't know where the name comes from and I have never heard it before, but I feel it is right for our son. "His name is Leeiss." I lean over to the newborn as Jerren holds him close. "Welcome to Elorcui, our home, Leeiss. You are nuetre filjo, our son."

"Nuetre filjo." Jerren smiles down at his son, proudly. Looking up to me, he grasps my hand tighter. Once again, his gaze finds our son's. "Welcome to your new home."

CHAPTER TEN

The Move

*N*ot long after the births of our sons, we move into Jaad's home. It is exceptionally comfortable for all of us.

If anyone had ever told me that I would be the mother to three boys, from three different versions of the same man, because of a single night, I would have laughed. It was something I had never imagined happening.

It doesn't matter to me that I will never see Earth, or the place I called home again. I will never feel the same sunsshine, or walk through the grass on Earth. I was with my family. This is my new home.

The nurseries have been finished for Lanon, Joeve, and Leeiss. The rooms are done in the same hues of gold and white as the rest of the house. There is a crib, changing table, small dresser, closet, and night table in each one.

Our bedroom, the one I share with my Mates is bigger, accommodating the four of us and our needs. On Elorcui, Pair Bondings are called Mates. In our case, I have three Mates and they have me. Our bed is the exact size we all need, as the men insist on sleeping with me. I am often spooned during the night by Kinim or Jerren or both. Kinim prefers sleeping on my left, as 'it is closer to the door'. It makes him more accessible to our sons. Jerren lies at my right, often laying his head on my breast and sighing contentedly. Thomael's favorite spot, whether we are having sex or not, is as close to the middle of my body as possible.

We spend several weeks falling into a daily routine. Jerren went back to the office where I was held. He is a man of importance in Elorcui, but never mentions his station. Only that he is needed and has to attend to business every day. When that is mentioned, my three Mates exchange glances, but never tell me what he does. He loves me and that is enough.

Kinim and Jerren love all of the boys as theirs. I saw it in their actions at their births and now see it through their expressions, as they hold each boy. Thomael favors our son, and that bothers me. How can someone show one child more love than the others around him? Being as all of the men are essentially the same, how can Thomael justify liking his Becoming's son over his son's from his other two Becomings? Joeve and Leeiss are his sons too.

Thomael, Kinim, and I care for the children during the day. At night, we all make sure our sons have what they need. There are stretches of time that all of the men are gone. They try to stagger their leaving, so I won't be alone with our sons, but it happens at times. I am fine with it, because I can bring them to our room and play with them, until they or I become exhausted. Then we all rest.

I begin creating pieces of art for our home. Mostly collages of our sons, with my Mates and myself. Even when the children are with their fathers or sleeping, I still want to stay busy. I want to wander the grounds of our spacious home, but can't. Again, I am kept at a distance from everything and everybody else.

Two months after our move, I begin to get even more restless. Being inside is confining and I want to be out, seeing the sights and visiting the peoples of my Mates' world. I want to taste the food from a street vendor or restaurant. I want to walk around and feel the sunsshine. I want to be free. As much as I love our home, I feel as if I have exchanged one gilded cage for another. This one more opulent and grand, but just as confining.

Another month passes and my libido begins returning. A fact that begins as a passing thought. I miss being with my Mates. I have never really been with Thomael, Kinim, or Jerren alone, and wonder what it will be like to have such personal time with them. My body begins to ache from the wanting, and soon becomes an almost incessant throbbing in the core of my being.

On Earth, I knew how to relieve myself when this happened. Now that I have Mates, surely one of them can take care of it for me. But how to get one of them alone? I was never good at seduction or flirting, so that is out. Maybe I should be more direct and tell them what I want? I can just imagine it now. I would walk into the room, where my Mates are playing with our sons, and announce that I am ready to make love. Would they fall over themselves, trying to get to me first or not care? Would they draw straws or suggest a game of rock, paper, scissors? Ugh! Maybe I should just save us all the embarrassment and take care of myself when I am alone. I decided that tonight, before my Mates come to our bed, I would retire early, and take care of myself. Yeah, that will happen. It will relieve my Mates of any awkward discussion.

Tonight, Jerren and I are in the family room, playing with the babies. I make the excuse that I am tired and kiss him and our sons good night.

As I am make my way through the foyer to the stairs, I hear Thomael and Kinim speaking quietly. Their tones are low, and as I move to listen, they quiet. I can still see their facial expressions, as if they are speaking out loud.

I bid them good night and see them slip into the family room. Thomael does not look happy.

Jerren catches up to me on the stairs. "Might I escort you to bed, my dear."

"I would love for you to do so, min eurozan." I hold out my arm and he slides his through it.

When the door shuts behind Jerren and I, he moves to me and draws a strand of hair between his fingers. "Sunsshine and honey." His green eyes find mine. "It's been over a thousand years, min eurozan."

Is he wanting...? Does he want me? I warm at the thought. It has been so long and I am ready to be loved. I will start with the one who holds my soul.

"It's like riding a bike," I drop my head just a little and wink at him. "Except I get to ride you."

I take his hand and lead him to our bed, kissing him tenderly as we go. This is the second time we have made love, but it is very much like the first. Jerren's loving is hesitant but sure. Strong, yet gentle. I let him take the lead and take his time as we make love. Before it is all over, I want to cry. This man, this Becoming, hasn't known me in over a thousand years. He has waited for me and never wanted to take a Mate, knowing I was coming for him. Now, he can have all of me. I love Jerren for his care of my heart.

When he begins snoring soundly, I curl into him and fall asleep.

Our lives continue on as usual. Jerren leaving for his office as the suns rise, while I and my Mates care for the children.

A week later, I begin my monthly cycles again. I have always been irregular and there is much pain each month. My Mates are considerate of my moods and cautious around my temper. Our sons fuss at their nursings, possibly because of the hormones coursing through my body. Thomael, Kinim, and Jerren hold our sons more, as I apologize for the children's behavior. Had I been on Earth, I would understand more about breastfeeding, but I am not.

Janele comes for a visit during that time. Away from my Mates, I discuss with her what is happening and how I am feeling. The children aren't happy with me. To be honest, I'm not happy with myself. But, for me, that isn't unusual. My hormones at this time are usually all over the place.

Before she leaves, she promises to return soon after she

has done some research. To my surprise, the very next day she returns with various kinds of information on how to help me with our sons during my cycles. That blessed Elorcuian is having a private session with my Mates, and then myself, on what to expect.

This cycle has lasted only five days and I am free of its curse for another twenty-something days. My libido kicks into overdrive. My body is ready for my Mates again, and it isn't shy about wanting them.

That very night, I make my way to our bedroom after dinner. Will my body control my thoughts and urges now? I stand on the balcony of our bedroom and stare out at the city, wishing one of my Mates will come to relieve me.

The door to our bedroom opens and I turn to see Kinim slip into the room. He shuts the door behind himself. "I wondered where you had gotten off to." He says, walking further into the room.

"It's been a long day. The children are growing and eating almost constantly. They need the nourishment. I love them, and will always give them what they need, but I need a few moments alone." I reply, watching the outside.

"Would you like me to leave?" He asks, not moving, but waiting for my answer.

"No." I say, and hear him walk to my side.

"We are as much help as we can be." He stops, glances at me for a moment, and then turns to the city.

I smile to him, and remember the old days. We are close, he and I, and I love that. "I know. Thank you." I move to him, and slip my arm through his. It's nice to instigate touch, as opposed to having someone have to touch me.

"You remember when I brought you here? I didn't want to leave you."

"You didn't." I say, moving closer to him, looking up into his handsome features. "I know now why you didn't. I was carrying your sons."

"Yes. I didn't know you could conceive our sons, when

we made love to you. We want you and the children to be safe and cared for. Jaad was our best choice in making sure both of those happened." He clears his throat. "I'm glad Jerren was your first after the birth of our sons. He has waited for you over a thousand years and needed you more than Thomael or myself." He half-turns, and catches my eyes with his. "For five days last week you bled. Janele says the bleeding might be a sign that you are not expecting Jerren's child."

"I don't think I am. I don't feel the way I did when I was pregnant." I watch the moonslight play across the grass. "Would that bother you if I was? The child would have been Jerren's."

"Jerren and I are One. His child would be mine and I would cherish it as my own. Do you not see that I treat Lanon and Leeiss the same as Joeve?"

"Yes, and I admire you doing so. You are love, and I am incredibly thankful for your heart."

We stand together in comfortable silence. The moons play across the yard in a brilliant display.

"Do you miss the times before, opposed to how we are now? When it was just you and I, or when you were with Thomael?"

"I do. Sometimes, and then I think of what I have now. I wouldn't trade that for anything." I reach up to unknot a bundle of muscles in my neck.

"May I?"

I nod my head.

He starts working his magic and smoothing out the knots. "Better?"

"Heavenly." I say, lolling my head from side to side. "Thank you." I move from his touch toward our bedroom. "Do you need something, Kinim?"

"I wanted to take care of you, min eurozan, but you wish to be left in peace." He starts toward the door. "I will go."

"The night in your hotel room." I say, quickly, not wanting him to leave. "Don't tell them, but thank you for being so beautifully gentle with me."

He stops, and clenches his fist. It's a Thomael move. "You are ours. It was our first night together." He turns and watches me, careful with his words. "I wanted to hold you in my arms while I took you, whisper my love as we completed one another."

"Thank you for your thoughtfulness."

Kinim turns back to the door.

"Min eurozan?" My Mate is here and we can be one.

He stops walking, but doesn't turn around.

"And if I said, I want. to feel your arms around me and hear your words of love again? What will you say?" I hold my breath, waiting to see what he does.

He pivots and crosses the room to take me in his arms. "I will do for you exactly what you want. I will be all that you need me to be. We will burn brightly, as twin flames and then merge to become one."

I lean forward. "Merge with me."

It takes no more prompting. He leans down to pick me up and takes me to our bed. We express our love in touches and quiet words.

Another week passes and I begin to feel the restlessness return. My body begins to ache and I need one of my Mates. It is a constant need. It wants to be quenched and is drawing me to touch and hold my Mates more. As I hug them, I turn my head to breathe them in deeply. I love to draw their scents into my nostrils. It floods my brain with a greater need for whomever I am holding, making me more aware of them. My blood is fueled, and I feel like a woman on fire.

The following morning, Jerren doesn't go into the office, but stays home with our sons. He and Kinim exchange looks at the breakfast table, but don't say anything, about whatever they are silently communicating. Occasionally, one or both of them eye Thomael, as he fidgets with his food. His restless energy is ready to be exhausted. I keep my legs together under the table, hoping that by pressing them together, it helps to alleviate the pressure. It doesn't, and I make eye contact only when necessary. The children have already been fed and are playing happily in their beds, waiting for us to come and retrieve them.

"It's beautiful outside today." I try not to sound envious and fail. My Mates and our sons could go outside anytime they wanted. "Why don't you take the children for some sunsshines?" A plan is already formulating in my mind. When they are gone, I shall go upstairs and lessen this insistence.

Thomael grips his fork, and I see his fingers turn white. Kinim and Jerren look to him, knowingly. Thomael relaxes his hand and nods once. The movement is barely perceptible, but I notice it.

"I think we shall, my dear. It's an excellent idea." Jerren says, finishing his food.

Kinim is already done eating. "The children have already eaten and have not been outside lately. We'll take them now." He nods at Jerren and Thomael.

Both men stand, as does Thomael.

I do as well. The rising internal temperature of my body is worse in the presence of my Mates. I try not to think about the time that Jerren and I or Kinim and I stole together in our room. But those memories surface, slamming forcefully into my brain.

I resist the urge to fan myself.

My Mates draw close and kiss me separately, and head off to get their sons ready for the day.

Well, that's great, I think. I should be rejoicing. I'm getting the "me time" that I want. But do I really want it? No, I think, and sink down into my chair.

Breakfast is a trial and I have hardly eaten. My body isn't craving the nourishing food that it should be, instead it craves one or all of my Mates that sat at the table. The need for them supersedes my empty stomach.

I stand, resolute. I will see them out the door with our sons and take care of what I must. Yes, I will be alright once they returned.

I just made my way to the foyer, when my Mates comes down the stairs with their sons. I've been blessed to have such excellent Mates, who care so much for their children.

"We're off." Kinim says, toting Joeve in his arms. I receive a kiss from him and they make their way out the front door.

"Until later, my dear." Jerren pecks me sweetly on the cheek and carries Leeiss outside to join Kinim and Joeve.

Thomael growls, quietly. "We'll see you later." He pulls me close and plunders my mouth with his. As he pulls back, I am flush. Lanon is watching us, a smile on his face. Like father, like son.

My Mate stomps across the threshold with our son. I jump when the door slams shut behind them.

I see I am not the only one with temper issues.

As I turn to begin my quiet time, the front door bangs open. Thomael strides in and leans down to carefully throw me over his shoulder.

"What are you doing?" I say, hitting his back, as I am carried up the stairs. "Where is Lanon?" I say, sitting up.

"Taking you to bed." He says, opening our door and tossing me on our bed. "Kinim and Jerren are taking care of him," he replies, descending upon me.

"What are you doing?" I ask, my hands on his shoulder as he begins to remove the clothing from my body.

"It's my turn." He peels the last of my clothing from me. His eyes following every valley and curve of my skin. "Mine."

Once again, he dives for me, but I hold him back. Every fiber of my being is screaming at me to have him.

"Your turn?"

He's like a bull, revving up for the charge. Pent up energy is pouring from him, ready to be consumed.

Thomael draws me close and I hear him lick his lips. "We've been Scenting you for days. Your body has been telling us that you need to be possessed, min eurozan. As Jerren has already had his turn with you and Kinim has pleased you as well, I feel it fair that I get to have you now."

The thought of him "having me" makes me swallow hard. Thomael doesn't do anything halfway, and he wants what he wants when he wants it. In short, he is a man, starving and I will be his meal. He'll be rough, pulling my hair and slapping my behind, as he takes his time having me any and every way he desires.

As we make love, my entire being is focusing on every part of him. I am not left wanting, as he pleases himself with me. He makes sure to satisfy me, washes my body, draws close to, and wraps himself around me. His expressive love leaves a path of loving destruction in its turbulent wake.

"Min eurozan," he breathes out quietly, and promptly falls asleep.

They've been Scenting me for days, I think as I lay with Thomael over me. And Thomael decided he is the one to have me? No discussion with Kinim or Jerren? Or has there been? They has been eyeing one another at the breakfast table. Maybe they are speaking to one another? Is it about the day, me, or both? Were they already planning to take the boys out, before I suggested it? Or did they agree to it because they know what I was going to do?

It made sense that they could read my mind. I had been "tuned" to their sons since they started speaking to me. They were in my womb at the time and were still developing, but that didn't hinder them from communicating from me.

Had my connection to their sons brought me into their minds too? Thomael, Kinim, and Jerren were, in essence, the same person. That meant their sons were brothers as well. If they are all the same people, in two different generations, then they are interconnected. I had already established the connection when the children began listening and speaking to me.

If that was the case, then my Mates and our sons, knew I was needing them again. The children were extra cooperative today, and Lanon was smiling as he and his father exited the door. Did they all already know Thomael would come back for me, as the rest of them continued on? Was this all prearranged before they walked out the front door?

I glance at Thomael, sleeping soundly. He had waited for Jerren and Kinim to have me. His very possessive nature would have demanded he be first. But he held himself back, allowing the others to have their turns with me. Now it is his turn to have me, and I wouldn't waste a moment of it.

Placing my hands under his shoulders, I carefully roll him over. He snores once and then falls back to sleep. I rise and slide down his body, ready to perform the same action on him that he loves to do to me.

Oh, yes. Our time together will be most memorable, I think, drawing close to the center of his body and opening my mouth. Most memorable for us both.

CHAPTER ELEVEN
My Exploration

I place my hands on my hips, turning to my Mates. We have eaten a light lunch and are inside the house. The family room has become one of our favorite places in the house as a family.

"I just want to go outside." I say, flinging a hand to the outdoors. "I've been in this house for months. If I don't see anything other than these blasted walls soon, I'm going to go mad." In truth, I am going a bit stir crazy. I need to go outside. Feel the breeze, the suns on my face, and the grass under my toes.

In my mind, my Mates had abruptly stop speaking to me. It wasn't too long ago that I found the "path" that my Mates use to speak to me and "tuned" into it. This surprised both myself and them, as we could now freely "speak" to one another, without being in hearing distance. On Earth, this wasn't a thing, but on Elorcui, Janele assures me, Mates should be able to do such things. And, oh, I do.

I am cut off from communication with them. Their eyes slide to one another, as if they are speaking, but they don't verbally say anything.

"Lovely." I almost roar. "You have all excluded me, again, from whatever conversation the three of you choose to have.

That's awesome!"

Tears threaten to spill from my eyes, but I hold them back. When they leave my mind, I am left with a crippling vacuum.

Jerren's and Kinim's arms come around me, but it is the latter Mate that speaks. "We don't mean to do that, my dear," he begins, and then flashes a look to Thomael.

I see my most possessive Mate shake his head. "I'm not done talking to you two." He continues blocking me out.

I knew it! I thought there were times they were speaking with one another.

Kinim's and Jerren's voices fill my head once more, but Thomael's is absent. I miss his voice even as I rejoice in hearing my other two Mates.

"We don't have visitors in Elorcui." Kinim says, but they are Jaad's words.

The thought of his voice surprises me. I immediately miss the Mate that I can never see again.

"We don't mean to hurt you, min eurozan." Jerren releases me, and Kinim pulls me close. "None of us ever mean you any harm. But we are One, and sometimes you will hear our other Becoming's words from us."

I already know that bit of information, but it stings, nonetheless. "I know, but he is a piece of my heart that I can never have back."

Thomael moves forward to stand in front of me, his fists at the sides. His eyes move back and forth between Kinim and Jerren. "You all know the risk we take."

Jerren "pushes" an apology into my mind and disconnects. His eyes flash to Thomael and Kinim. Once again, he reconnects to my mind and smiles again. "Please forgive me, my dear. Now that I know how you feel when we leave you, I shall endeavor to be more sensitive."

"If you can tell me why I can't go outside, I will feel better."

Jerren steps back to me and takes one of my hands.

Kinim takes my other and looks to Thomael.

"If you both want her to know, then she will know all of it. Is that what you want?" He looks from Jerren to Kinim.

They both nod their head at the exact same time.

His hand reaches out and pulls me from them. I'm taken to the couch with him and he sits, pulling me down to his lap. "Then I will tell our history in the way I choose." With one hand, I am urged to sit face to face with him. It's an intimate position that we have been in before. Any other time, I would have burned for him. This is not the time. He is going to regale me with Elorcui's history and I am attentive.

"Our city – our world –was not always a peaceful one." He begins, setting his hands on my waist. "Many, many years ago, there were wars, famine, and destruction. There were those in need and those who had abundance. Whomever was in need, had very little. There are those who worked hard for what they could earn and wanted to hold on to what they had. Whomever had the abundance wanted to keep all they had and take from those who had next to nothing. It became so bad, that most of Elorcui was exceedingly poor and just a small percentage had practically everything. After much discussion by our cities government, we decided to take our resources and divide them equally among its citizens. The wealthy, most of whom had been given everything their entire lives, balked at the idea. Those who were working to hold on to what they had, thought that it was an excellent idea. After the judicious decision, there were no more classes. All worked for an equal share. No one was given more than anyone else. In a single one of your months' time, all classes and divisions were erased. If one wants something, they have to help society in some way or another. Thus, it ensures our society continues. Our leadership is held in place rather precariously, because we depend on each other for everyday life."

I have watched Thomael's eyes the entire time he has spoken. "I don't contribute anything to your society. If I can get out and help, I would feel a part of it. Like I am one of you."

Kinim tugs me over into his arms. At one point, he and Jerren had come to sit on the couch with us. I sit with my legs across his lap and he pulls me close. "You are a part of our lives just by being, min eurozan. You've started to create art, and our home is graced with pictures of all of us and our sons. If you would like to contribute in a way that will help our family, continue creating the art you love. We will take it to the marketplace and have someone barter or trade for what we need. You do not have to do this, but if you wish, please do so."

I look up to him. "But why can't I take them there?"

He exchanges a look to my other Mates. Jerren and Thomael withdraw from my mind. Jerren is the only one to apologize before he does so.

"Why can't I go the marketplaces and learn how to barter for what we need? I can still do this and take care of our sons." I glance to Thomael and Jerren. "I can take our sons with me and sell my art." Kinim withdraws from my mind and I am left alone. "No." Tears well in my eyes, and I wipe them away before they fall. "Don't all of you leave me. Just tell me why."

Jerren reaches for me and Kinim releases me go to him. I sit down beside my Mate. "There are some who resisted how we had chosen to set up our society. Most eventually came on board, but those who chose not to, became outcasts. Of their own free will, they left the city to live outside of its borders. They don't want to conform to our ways or our laws. They live the way they want." He takes his hand in mine. "We once allowed visitors from other worlds in our city. They came only to take what they could. We had to fight with them, and almost lost. In fact, many lives were lost to the battles before it was all over. Once they all left us, we had to make a new declaration, saying that we wouldn't allow visitors to our city."

Thomael stands, restless now. "Any visitor."

His eyes find mine and they are hard. "That's why Jaad

told you what he did."

"When you were held in my office," Jerren continues, "we made sure to mask your otherworldly scent. Elorcuians don't have the same scent as you. Your essence is more pure, natural. You would have been Scented and an alarm would have been raised."

This is a lot to process! "You kept me in your office, because I didn't smell like your people." I could have been killed, most likely, or worse.

"Elorcuians can only conceive children when they are bonded Mates." Thomael offered.

Jerren drew my attention. "When you went to Kinim and Thomael came to you, if they had made love to you, you wouldn't have conceived. They loved you, yes, but they were not Mated to you." He sighs, heavily. "When I came to you, wanting you as they did, in the timeline we are in now, we are already Mated. I was the one to spark the Bond. It isn't in our biology to allow conception unless we are Mated. That makes you, Judin, very special to us."

"What if I find myself with children again?" My eyes catch theirs.

To their credit, they don't look away.

Kinim draws close and take my hands again. "All life is precious to us." He smiles softly. "If you conceive with any or all of us again, then we will welcome those children with open arms."

My Mates exchange looks. Their eyes comeback to mine. Jerren speaks. "We are exactly who we are with you because this is the way we were made for you."

"You are a gift to us. Because of that, we want to give ourselves to you." Kinim stands and catches me up in his arms. "You have a larger part to play in our lives, min eurozan. We feel that in every molecule of who we are."

"Christan said you aren't omniscient or omnipresent."

"True." Jerren confirms, coming close to us. "We see the universe and all that can be at the present. Possible futures are laid out before us, with an incalculable number of variables. But you, my dear, are at the center of almost everyone here."

"That still doesn't answer the question as to why I can't go outside." My Mates exchange quiet sighs. "My pheromones can be masked or covered, can they not? I can take our sons with me, in my arms if need be, everywhere I go. Or do they smell like me? Like an otherworlder?" If they do, it will put them in danger as they grew. "Do they, Kinim? They don't, right?" Tears well in my eyes. What if I have put my hearts in danger just by birthing them?

"No, Judin," Jerren begins, "they are made in your body with a mix of our DNA." He exchanges looks with Thomael and Kinim. "But our DNA repressed yours. It became dominant and took almost every aspect of being from Earth from them."

Click! Another piece snaps into place. "Which is why I don't see myself in them." I try not to be sad at the prospect that my own sons will never look anything like me. The thought is selfish, but I had nurtured them within me for months. I want a piece of me still around when I'm not. Now, I will never have that.

"The repression was necessary, so that when the time comes they can fully integrate into our society." Jerren explains.

It doesn't help. An inexplicable sadness washes over me. There will be nothing of me, once I am no more. Down deep, my own DNA cries out at the injustice of it all.

Kinim turns me towards him. "They will have your mannerisms and expressions. They will know your love and who you are as their mother. Everything about you since their mind formed, has been captured in their memories." His hands gently cup my shoulders. "Joeve may one day have your care for others with the same feelings you possess." He casts a glance to Thomael. "Lanon may one day have the same fire as his mother, and that will surprise Thomael." I look to Jerren. "And his mind can be as sharp as yours, as he duels wits with his father." His eyes find mine again. "Our sons may not, in looks, be like you, but they will be you in personality. If your time comes and we have to tell you good-bye." He stops as Thomael growls loudly and Jerren menacingly steps forward. "We will see you in them." His hands caress my face and my Mates draw close, pressing against me. Kinim's fingertips touch my face. "But, min eurozan, as One, we do not see that time happening. Not in Thomael, mine, or Jerren's time."

"But time can change what you all see, can it not? If a variable falls out of place or is added?" I ask, looking to my Mates.

Their eyes meet mine.

It is Thomael who speaks. "The variables are always changing, yes. And we don't see everything. But we see what we can to keep you safe. In Elorcui, you have the best chance for survival. None of us ever want to lose you, but what we have seen tells us you will leave."

"But I don't want to leave it, I want to live in your city, not just exist with everything around me."

"Our city." Thomael insists, firmly. "Elorcui is as much your city as it is our sons. And, you, min eurozan, will be with us all for a long time to come."

"How did you mask my scent when I was in your office?" I ask Jerren, whose mind whirls to answer.

"I knew you as my Mate. My body secreted an extra hormone that masked yours."

I cock my head to the side. "How did you know it would do that?"

His eyes met Kinim's. "The night Kinim came to tell me about you, he brought an article of your clothing. It isn't the same as having you in the room. I took it across every piece of furniture in the room and had Christan come into the room. As he stepped in, I saw him begin to take a breath. I felt my blood surge. When he exhaled, I asked him if anything seemed off. He looked around the room and inhaled again. He replied that all is the same and I dismissed him."

"So, he didn't scent me?" I brought a hand to my chin.

101

"You said you 'felt your blood surge'?"

"Yes."

"I wonder if you released your scent to mask mine then." I postulate, and step out from them all.

They went back to their children.

I had another thought.

"When I am with each of you," I clear my throat, as their eyes meet mine, "do I smell like myself or who I'm not with?"

My Mates look at each other.

Thomael answers for them. "Your scent is your own. I don't smell Kinim or Jerren on you."

He would be the one to know. By the time we are through, I was sure we had Scented each other.

Kinim and Jerren nod their heads in agreement.

A curious question comes to mind. "And when you are all with me?"

They exchange looks again.

"On that one occasion that we had you as ours, I did Scent Thomael and Kinim on you. But my focus was on making you happy and bringing you as much pleasure as I could." Jerren said, watching me. "What are you thinking, my dear?"

"I wonder if our sons can do the same thing their fathers do? I can take our sons." I begin, and press on. "Mothers, fathers, and caregivers on Earth would carry the babies in homemade carriers. I have even seen one before that holds three babies." My Mates look skeptical. "I can have Lanon in front," I hold out my hands to where he would ride. "And Joeve on my hip." I indicate where he would be. "And Leeiss on my back. Surely, carrying them on me, would mask my scent."

"What if they don't and you are Scented by someone from outside the city?" Thomael asks, watching me.

I cock my head at Jerren. "They are allowed inside?"

"Of course," he answers, playing with our son, "as long as they follow the rules."

"If our sons can mask my Scent in the carriers, I would

have no problem." I say, proudly.

"That's a big if." Thomael stands and crosses his arms, causing his muscles to bulge.

"We can, at least try it." I say, hopefully.

There is silence in the room and in my mind. They are speaking to one another again. I hated being left out of the conversation.

Kinim features are resigned.

Thomael does not look happy.

Jerren appears confident. "We'll try it."

I clap my hands and bounce on my toes.

"But, we will all go out – together – as a family." Jerren continues. "As One. If anything should happen, I shall intervene while Thomael and Kinim bring you and our sons' home." Jerren is firm in his decision.

Yay! I think, happily hugging all of my Mates. "Thank you!" I get to go outside after many months of being cooped up.

Their expressions don't change.

"I'll draw up a pattern and make the triple carrier." I tell Kinim. "It will be strong enough to carry our sons." I tell Thomael. "And it will work." I tell Jerren. "You'll see. I just need the materials and soon our sons will have their carrier."

CHAPTER TWELVE
The Vision

*T*he morning of my visit to the Elorcui dawns brightly. The suns are shining through our bedroom window, illuminating the room in a bright glow. I feel like a kid at Christmas! I finally get to see my Mates city!

I gently push Kinim to lay beside me and Jerren off of my chest. He moves close to spoon my body. Thomael is in his customary position, just below my waist.

"Okay, guys," I speak into their mind. "I would like to sit up. You all promised I can see the city after the carrier is finished. It's done and I am itching to go."

"Our city," Thomael states, telepathically. "Elorcui is your home, too."

There are times we have given up speaking aloud and think into one another's mind. This is one of them.

Kinim yawns in my thoughts. "You've done an excellent job on our sons' new carrier, min eurozan."

My reassuring Mate. "I love you." I think only to Kinim.

He smiles in his half sleep. "And I you, Judin."

"I know you are excited," Jerren interjects, "but it is still early. The marketplaces are still being set up. Those who will be bartering won't be ready, for at least another couple of Earth hours."

It does irritate me so that my Mates would equate their time with that of Earth. I want to be like them and do what they do. Still being treated like an otherworlder is frustrating. My Mates do it to help me understand time and such, but I still want to be more like them.

"We shall leave when we are ready, min eurozan." Jerren reaches over and pulls my back to his front. "Rest for a while longer. Our sons are still sleeping."

I glance to the screens across from our bed. Yes, our little ones are still angels, resting for our big day.

"They know about our outing?" I ask my Mates, who are already dozing again.

"Yes," Kinim answers, pressing himself against my front. "Please, go back to sleep."

Thomael sits up and glares at me. "Well, I'm awake." He grabs my hips and turns me to lay flat on my back. "I don't know about the rest of you, but I am going to start my morning right." His head dips to my middle as Kinim and Jerren move back to my side.

I feel their breaths move across my neck and chest.

Thomael is my amorous Mate. He thinks about how he can take me. Often. The only time he doesn't ponder it is when he is with our son.

As his teeth, mouth, and tongue ravish me, Kinim and Jerren add their own touches and kisses to my body. To be loved by three Mates is glorious and I revel in our time together. They are all speaking words of love sensually to me, as Thomael continues pleasing my core. I am ever so thankful that they can speak to one another without me, as when one of them instigates a lovemaking session that all four of us attend.

It always ended the same way. We all are covered in sweat and the smell of one another, although my Mates only have an interest in me. When one of them can't stand it any longer, they take my body to claim as their own. I climax to the end of myself and then they lose themselves in me. There really isn't a reasoning to who has preference. It is always only the one of them who capture my body, while my other Mates heighten my pleasure.

Thomael rips his mouth from my privates and pinpoints a look to me. "You won't bathe."

Kinim and Jerren are kissing and touching all over my body and in my hair. The only part they don't touch is where Thomael currently resides.

"Your other two Mates will ejaculate themselves on your body and you will caress it into your skin." He slides into me. "I will remain inside of you today, as we walk through the streets. Our sons and your Mates shall be your essence."

We continue loving one another. I come to the end of myself and Thomael follows, laying his head on my soft stomach.

"You will do all that you are told to do, while we are in the city." His arms come around my hips as he draws himself close to me.

Kinim and Jerren stop writhing. I feel their essence on my skin, from where they have come to the end of themselves.

Jerren leans close to kiss my lips sweetly and smiles down at me. "You are our life, min eurozan." He lies down and draws close to my side again.

Kinim touches my face with his fingertips. "We will do all that we must to keep you and our sons safe." His kiss is hard, but not rough like Thomael's. He curls into my side and closes his eyes.

I know they mean well, my Mates. I will never knowingly do anything to allow myself to be taken from them or our sons. They are allowing me this trip into Elorcui. The least I can do is whatever they think will bring me the most safety.

"I'll do whatever you say," I speak out loud to my Mates, wanting to reassure them that the day will go off without a hitch. "You are all my loves. Thank you for allowing me go out today."

Jerren's arm come around my middle, just above

Thomael's head.

Kinim lays an arm across my chest, just above Jerren's head.

It's too cute, I think, weirdly. They look like sleeping kittens, huddled up around their momma. Needing her love and nurturing support.

But looks are deceiving. I know that they are fierce, predatory tigers, ready to pounce, ripping apart their adversary to protect what is theirs.

I have seen it with my own eyes with Kinim. Kinim, while my most affectionate Mate, has done some justifiably horrible things in cold and methodical ways. He is anyone's worst nightmare if they threatened what is his.

Jerren is Kinim, in another Becoming, and has had over a thousand more years to take that internal savagery and tame it. I am sure, if pushed, he can be as disconnected in his violence as Kinim has been. Maybe even more so.

Thomael is, well, Thomael. I am sure he can rip anything or anyone apart with his bare hands, if necessary, if it meant keeping his loved ones safe. His life is about protecting and keeping what is his. If threatened, I would bet he would strike without hesitation or remorse. He wouldn't be as... subtle... as Kinim or even Jerren, but he would be just as terrifying.

If they all worked together against what they perceived is a threat, they could bring down worlds.

My rational mind, if I listen to it, is probably telling me to run, but I don't want to. This is my home and these are my Mates. I would give my life protecting them and our sons. If they will do the same for me, then I will do so for them.

I lift my hips to bring Thomael closer to me. If they want me, then I will be whatever they need to be for them. Do whatever is asked, so that they will be satisfied. They are all my hearts and I will move the heavens to make sure they feel loved. Not because I fear them, but because my love for them exceeds anything else, save for that of our sons.

I bring my hands to Jerren's essence and rub him into my

skin. I do the same for Kinim's. If they want me to smell like them, then I will.

They nestle close, pulling me closer to them. I bring my arms around Jerren and Kinim.

Jerren moves his head while on my chest and opens his eyes, looking into mine. He lifts his hand and draws it down before my eyes. It is a trick Jaad has used often on me. "Sleep."

I don't resist the push to fall into the dark abyss of dreaming. My Mates and children wait for me. I welcome their love with open arms.

***

When I next open my eyes, my Mates are climbing out of our bed. I get an unobstructed view of them as they start their morning routine. Their forms are sleek, muscles flexing on Thomael as he unwraps a towel from his clean body and begins to dress for the day. I hear the water turn off and Kinim stepping out of the bath. Soon, he will select his clothes. Jerren is standing unclothed in front of the screens, watching our sons coo happily in their cribs. My Mates move around one another unashamedly. They are the same person, so maybe that is why it doesn't bother them to do so.

I'm not quite there yet. I always grab some sort of covering to hide my body when I rise from bed.

"Why do you do that?" Thomael asks, without speaking aloud. His eyes catch mine as he slips on his elastic pants. The same type he always wears.

"Jealousy, I suppose." I say, sitting up in bed and bringing the covers with me as I do.

"We don't feel jealousy the same way you do, Judin." Kinim offers, coming around the corner of the closet with his clothes. Kinim wore the same outfit everyday too. "Thomael, Jerren, and I are the same person. We can be selfish with you and want you over the other at times, but we are unable to be jealous of one another."

I look to Jerren, while speaking to Kinim. Thomael can hear my thoughts too. "So, if I walk over to Jerren without anything covering me..."

Thomael is almost dressed. He strides over to our bed and pulls back the covers. His arms slide under me. Neither Kinim nor Jerren move as Thomael handles me.

"We all share you equally and appreciate your form, whenever we get a chance to see it."

I am deposited by Jerren's side, while Thomael goes back to getting dressed.

"He's absolutely right, my dear." Jerren reaches out an arm and brings me to his side. "We wouldn't mind at all if, once our sons are asleep for the night, if you walked around our home without any clothes on." He turns to smile down at me, then looks back to our sons.

Well, that answers that question.

"You keep looking at them," I say, watching him. "Is something wrong?"

"Not at all." He smiles down at me again. "I hear our son the same as the day he is born, but Lanon's and Joeve's voices have been... turned down." When he frowns, I see Thomael flash him a look of concern, and Kinim comes to stand beside us. He's dressed now.

"I still hear them all." Kinim says, looking to Thomael.

Thomael nods his head. "As do I."

"You're new," I start, trying to reassure him, but not quite sure how. "Maybe things are still adjusting for you?"

My Mates withdraw from my mind. Kinim wraps an arm around my waist, resting it on top of Jerren's. Thomael moves close to us.

"What?" I ask, watching them as they speak to each other, without me hearing. "What are you all talking about?"

I start to move out of their grip, but they tighten it. Thomael moves to me.

"You're frightening me," I say, watching them. Their eyes move to each other quickly, facial expressions almost

110

constantly changing. "Stop!"

They all snap back into my mind.

"We don't mean to frighten you, my dear." Jerren is trying to be reassuring.

It doesn't work.

"We are just postulating as to why Jerren isn't hearing Joeve and Leeiss the way he should." Kinim offers, looking to Jerren.

"And?" I ask, looking to each of my Mates. "Is something wrong with Leeiss, Jerren?" My eyes settle on him. "What's wrong with our son?" I begin to tremble where I stand. Should I go and get him? I reach out to him with my mind, but he is happy and not in pain. Is it something internal that Jerren can sense, but I can't?

"You're shaking." Thomael moves to stand directly behind me, pulling me into his embrace. I feel his warmth, but it isn't helping me.

"Min eurozan?" I ask, my eyes bearing into Jerren's. "Please. Speak to me."

Kinim moves to my side and curls into my body. His arms comes around my waist, as the three of us watch Jerren.

"Min eurozan?" I say, quietly, looking to my love. I move to throw myself into his arms, but am held back by my other Mates. "Let me go."

He finally turns to me. His hands come to my shoulders, bringing me close. My other Mates have followed my trek. "Our son is fine, Judin," he says, trying to reassure me.

"Then why the eerie silence? Please, speak to me." I'm begging him now. I need to know what is happening.

"We talked about the variables that may happen." He begins, still trying to reassure me.

"Yes." I answer, waiting.

"One has come into being."

Tears fall from my eyes. "What does that mean?"

"It means that there is an instability in the universe and anything can happen." Kinim supplies, still watching Jerren.

"What do we do?"

"We don't do anything. Everything is already set into motion. We continue with our day." Jerren nods his head. Thomael reluctantly steps back and Kinim moves to the side.

"Are the children safe?" I need to know if something is going to happen to them. They have to be protected above all else.

"You and the children will be kept safe," Jerren says, withdrawing from my mind and flashing a look to my other two Mates. "I need to get ready for the day, my dear." He leans down kissing me sweetly on the cheek, then goes into the bath.

I stand in our bedroom, watching as he leaves. "Something is going to happen, isn't it?" I ask, not really looking at Thomael or Kinim. "It's something that neither of you can change, too." I feel this ominous something vibrate in my body. "What is it?" I want to bring my arms around my body to shield myself from it, but my Mates continue holding me tight.

My perfect day outside is being overshadowed by something inevitable.

Kinim tilts his head down to me. "Do you feel it, min eurozan?"

"Yes." I look to Thomael. He will always keep me safe. Won't he? "I once had a tuning fork in my hand as it was struck. It vibrated so quickly that I couldn't keep track of it. I could feel its movement, but not see it. That is how my cells feel in my body."

Thomael wraps his arms around my shoulder and pulls me close.

Kinim secures his hands to my hips.

"You are becoming more like us, Judin. What you feel is a small part of how we do. Do you see anything? In your mind's eye?" Thomael's eyes bore into mine.

"No. It's just a feeling. And not a good one." My eyes slide to where Jerren is showering.

"Jerren." Kinim says, breathing out. "This is about him."

"Yes." I confirm, looking back to Kinim. "Something is going to happen to my love."

"Nothing permanent is going to happen to Jerren as long as we can help it, Judin. He is who we will be, and you have borne us sons." His eyes find Kinim's and come back to me. "Our future is in the two of you and our sons."

"And you are all my future. I wouldn't be here, we wouldn't have our sons, if it wasn't for the three of you. Please. Don't take my future from me. I love you all." I say, reaching behind me and bringing Kinim close. My other arm reaches for Thomael and pulls him close. "What do we do?"

Their arms come around me, keeping me close.

"We don't change any plans. Every possible future leads to whatever is going to happen. Nothing can change this course now." Thomael says, tightening his embrace.

"We will be more vigilant with you and children." Kinim draws closer to me, too. "Nothing will happen to the four of you."

The morning started out so great, and then nosedived. I don't want anything to happen to Jerren, but I know that something will. And the three of us are powerless to change it.

CHAPTER THIRTEEN
The City

"**D**ress now," Thomael says, pulling out of my embrace. "Kinim and I will take care of our sons. When you and Jerren are ready, meet us downstairs for breakfast." He pulls me close, kissing me roughly. "No washing us from you. Don't add any perfumes either."

"Yes, sir." I say, moving from him and towards my closet. "Anything else?" I want today to be perfect, not only for myself but my family.

"Just love us, min eurozan." Kinim comes by for a quick kiss and then is out the door with Thomael.

"Forever." I breathe to the air, knowing they all hear the thought before it is spoken aloud.

When I hear the shower stop, I turn to see Jerren stepping out of it. I watch him dry off and throw the towel into the chute.

My Mate is everything to me, and I want to show him the love I have.

He walks out of the bath completely naked. He, like my other Mates, always wears the same clothes every day. It should be annoying, but it isn't. The sameness is comforting.

"I love you," I say, and watch him stop.

He walks into the closet. "Is something the matter, min

eurozan?"

"We've had months to get to know one another, but it's not been enough time." I move to stand in front of him. He brings his fists to his sides, but isn't gritting his teeth like Thomael. "I want to know so much more about you." I bring my hand to his chest, running it from his collarbone to navel. "I know the taste of your skin. But we have only begun to love. I've had what seems like a lifetime with Thomael and Kinim. It seems like I've only begun with you."

"We will have our lifetime too, Judin. Do not worry about that."

I glance outside and instinctually know it's been a good hour since our romp on our bed. "Thomael said I can't wash myself or add any perfumes, but he didn't say anything about adding any more scents in my body." I drop my gaze, and bite my lip, walking slowly around his body. His form is magnificent, and is mine. I want to possess him.

I lift my hands to trace the hills and valleys of his back. He's warm and muscular like Thomael. He's taller and lankier than Kinim. I imagine Jaad would have been rounder, softer than the Mate in front of me. I take my time to admire his back side, all the way down to his feet.

"Are you trying to seduce me, min eurozan?" He asks, tightly.

"Is it working?" I shoot back, as I move back around him. He's not fully erect. I'll need to step this up a bit.

"You have my complete attention, my dear."

Oh, how I love it when one of my Mates bring another's words into play. "Not yet." I murmur, taking his hand. "I have been thinking…"

His hand wraps around mine, tenderly. "I know you have. And you have the most tempting thoughts. Ones that won't take us to the city any time soon."

"Is that a problem?" It is my turn to bring a Mate's words back. These were Kinim's to me when he returned from his Becoming.

"I don't have an issue with it, but I know you are eager."
He's watching me now, perfectly aware of what I want to do.
"The question is: are you willing to wait a bit longer?"

I begin to walk to our bed and he follows. He sits down
on our bed, waiting for me to continue.

My knees hit the floor in front of him. "As Thomael, you
have my body. As Kinim, you have my heart. As Jaad, you have
my mind. Now that you are Jerren, you have my soul. I have
seen four of your Becomings and I'm not sure how many you
have left. But, I have nothing left to give your future selves,
other than what you already own."

"The only thing we want is your love. You have our
undying self forever, min eurozan." He says, as he brings his
fingertips to my cheeks.

"I've never tasted you." I relish his touch, wanting more
of him. "I know you probably need a recovery time and I want
to give that to you, before I have you."

He's not surprised. I have already pictured myself doing
the same thing to him that Thomael adores having me do.

I glance down to see I have his full attention now.
"Thomael is inside me. You and Kinim are on my body." My
eyes meet his now. "But I want your taste in my mouth today.
I want the memories of satisfying you, as we walk the streets."

"We have a lifetime to do what you wish." He says, but
doesn't move from our bed or me. "We do not have to do this
now."

"But I want to do it now." I search my mind and find
that my other two Mates are playing happily with our sons.
They are fully aware of what is happening between Jerren
and myself. "The children are with their fathers and Leeiss is
content. I say now is the best time."

Jerren leans his elbows back on our bed, his expression
changing. "If you are doing this because of what is coming...?"

"I'm doing this because I love you, and because I want
to please you. In pleasing you, I also please myself. Not in
the same way, but I get to bring you such great joy." I smile,

teasingly at him. "Would you deny me happiness, by denying yourself?"

His hands reach out and his fingers slide into my hair. "If you feel the need to please me, my dear, then I will not deny you what you wish." He pulls my head closer between his thighs. "By all means, please yourself until your heart is content."

I open my mouth to receive him, as he trembles beneath my touch.

***

Later, we step down the stairs speaking quietly with one another. Jerren is more relaxed than I have ever seen him. His grin is wide and I am secured at his side. We stride into the breakfast room and he pulls out my chair.

"My dear."

I move to stand in front of the chair and sit when it presses against the back of my knees. "Thank you, sir."

As Jerren takes his seat, I notice our sons are already dressed for the day. Their carrier is sitting beside their cribs.

"And thank you both for getting them ready to go out." I say to my other Mates.

"As you and Jerren were busy..." Thomael begins, Kinim throws him a look.

"We were only thinking of having everything prepared for our departure this morning," Kinim continues, smoothly. "We know you have been eager," he pauses, knowingly, "for this day. Very exuberant to finally be able to do what you have wanted."

Thomael begins eating his breakfast, quietly.

Jerren is still smiling from ear to ear, as he starts eating his food.

I meet Kinim's gaze. "One of things I've been wanting to do." I have not been intimate in the same way with him, as I had with Thomael or Jerren. "But that will happen. Soon."

Kinim's right eyebrow arches up and his full lips spread into an easy smile. "I look forward to it." With that, he digs into breakfast.

We eat quickly, speaking to one another and the children, then proceed to leave.

Our home sits away from, but still inside, the city limits. My hope is that we walk all the way there, but that hope is dashed when Jerren speaks.

"As this is our first outing as a family, I have, what Judin terms "the flying machine" ready for us." He opens the door and we step into a larger version of the half helicopter, half airplane machine. On their backs, my Mates are carrying a small pack of necessities for their son. In their arms are their offspring.

Nerves kick in, as I sit to watch my Mates play with our sons. How would this all work? What if I need to feed them while we are away? If they need changed?

"We have prepared for all of that." Kinim answers in my mind for all to hear. "Our society is open and accepting to all children. Many Mates who have children take them to work with them every day. You will see a few mothers and fathers with them on their persons, carrying them much like you will our sons."

"You allow Mates to bring babies to work with them?" I address the question to Jerren.

"Our society is set up with babies and small children in mind. They are cared for and nurtured by all around them. Both Mates have to work to maintain their livelihood and to keep our society productive." He answers, he gazes and smiles upon our son.

"If we need to take care of our sons' needs, in any way, there would be no judgment or criticisms?"

"No." Thomael chimes in. "There may be some curious glances, as babies in Elorcui are rare."

Rare? "Why?"

"Because of our long lifespans." Kinim offers, stretching

out his arms to hand me our son.

I gladly accept him and bring him close to me, kissing him on the cheek. He's so perfect!

"We have no need to procreate because we Become. Babies and children are precious as they aren't common and are treated with respect and care."

I hadn't thought about there not being children in Elorcui. On Earth, little people are almost everywhere. "And if there are some who are overly curious?"

Three heads swivel to me. Their eyes intense.

Thomael is ready to answer my question, but Kinim beats him to it.

"Then we shall politely inform them that they are infringing upon our lives and ask them to maintain distance."

"Especially since you are from Earth." Thomael inhales, deeply. "You smell exactly like myself, Kinim, and Jerren. Add our sons to your scent, and no one will have any doubts you are from Elorcui."

"If that were to happen, I will summon our transportation home, and deal with any infraction that may occur. Thomael and Kinim will make sure you and our sons are taken home. I would follow when I could." Jerren glances to a sign over the door. "We are here."

I hand Joeve to Kinim. "We need to strap the children in."

We had practiced at home on how we would put on and secure the children in the harness. I strap it on, clicking the buckles and tightening the straps. One by one, each of our sons are added and secured. Soon, I have three small lives secured to my body.

"They are heavy," I say, accepting their weight as part of my day out. "But we are ready. Let's go explore our world."

Thomael smiles and kisses my lips. "Now you are getting it." He adjusts the hat on Lanon's head. Our son wiggles to the side and makes a face at his father.

I smile at their interaction.

Kinim grins reassuringly to me. "Ready when you are." Joeve is dutifully wearing the hat his father placed on him.

It's too cute!

Jerren secures Leeiss's hat and offers me his arm, stepping close to my left side. I have Lanon in the front, facing out, able to see what is in front of us. Joeve is on my right hip, smiling up at me. Leeiss is on my back, gurgling happily.

"Shall we, my dear?"

"Yes," I say, quietly, and then repeat louder. "Yes."

As the door begins to open, my Mates come around us. I know that they will take care of our sons and myself, if necessary.

I relax, secure in their love, and ready myself to begin a day of adventure.

CHAPTER FOURTEEN
The City Part II

*T*he door softly hits the green grass and the sunslight floods our view. We step out, moving as one, onto the grass and the door closes behind us.

I am finally outside! Lifting my head, I feel the suns on my face and yearn to take off my shoes and rub my feet on the grass.

"This is heavenly." I speak to my Mates' minds. "This is exactly what I've been needing."

They smile at my joy.

I begin to feel a slight prickly sensation on my skin. It's as if my pores are "opening" to receive what the sunslight is offering.

"We aren't particularly vulnerable to the rays in the same way as those from Earth." Kinim begins as we walk. "Our bodies adjust to the surroundings and accept what good it offers. Your body is changing, becoming like ours. This is how we feel when we step onto a new world. Some external changes are more intense and some less."

A long street with carts, wheel barrels, and tables are lined along it. I can see clothing swatches of all colors and patterns, smell the food cooking, and hear the people speaking. English?

"You heard English in my office." Jerren speaks into my mind only. "You perceive what you understand."

"Do you hear them in Elorcuian?" I ponder, not turning to him as we walk.

"I do." His other hand pats mine that lies on his arm. "Do not fret. We are here."

What would happen if they weren't? Would I or our sons be in danger? How would I defend them?

"In the best way you know how." Thomael speaks in my mind. "But that will never be the case, min eurozan. You are ours to love and protect." He bites the last part out, ready to do whatever is necessary, whenever it is called upon him.

"Relax, Judin." Kinim "pushes" into my mind.

I want to have a good day with my family, so I accept the suggestion. My limbs release their pressure and I feel good.

"Thank you, my love." I say, only to Kinim, smiling at him.

"You're always welcome." He grins back and then turns his focus to the people going to and fro. "Ready to plunge in?"

"I am." I reply to my Mates.

The children are happily chatting to one another, myself, and their fathers. I remember Leeiss is quieter now to his father and pull Jerren close.

"I love you." I speak aloud, softly to him.

"I know you do, my dear." He chuckles, quietly. "You made that plainly clear this morning." I see into his mind and the memories he has of our time together.

Thomael's memories transform, for just a second, to what he and I share. Our time during that activity is completely different than what Jerren and I have done. Thomael is insistent and demanding, and I love it.

Kinim's grin widens, happy at our loves.

As we move into the crowd, I feel my Mates stop simultaneously. Their eyes close for just a fraction of a second, and then open. Our sons repeat their actions at the same time.

The citizens continue browsing as we pass.

"What was that?" I ask, trying to appear as if this is a normal shopping day, speaking to my Mates and children in our minds.

"Mine." I hear Thomael and Lanon repeat. One out loud and the other in my mind.

"You're our heart." Kinim murmurs out loud and Joeve speaks into my mind.

Again, my Mate speaks quietly and our son in my thoughts.

"We have taken further precautions to mask your scent, momma." Leeiss says, looking directly at me.

His father continues. "This morning's lovemaking was to ensure you contained our Scent – in every way possible. But we took another step to make sure you aren't detected."

I take a deep breath and smell only my Mates and our sons. Their scents hung in the air around us. "Is that why I can Scent you all so distinctly?"

"Yes, mommy." Kinim's son replies. "We want to keep you safe."

"Thank you, my loves." I purr and my Mates move closer to me.

As we move together, down the golden streets of Elorcui, I am in awe. Everything imaginable is available in the long strip. Food, clothing, housewares, services, and other manner of objects are being bartered and traded for what the buyer needs.

"Do you want anything, my dear?" Jerren leans close to me, whispering.

"No, thank you." I reply, smiling at my Mate. His arm is still through mine and we are all still together.

At the end of the long street, there are several spacious benches. As we near them, our sons begin to fuss.

"My son is hungry." Thomael chimes in.

"As is Joeve and Leeiss." Kinim adds. "Please sit, min eurozan, and we will remove them from the carrier so that you may feed them."

Jerren chooses a bench with no occupants and my Mates carefully extract their sons from the carrier. I miss their weight as I remove the carrier and lay it off to the side.

A male Elorcuian sits on the bench away from us. He has what looks to be a turkey leg and is enjoying the meal.

In my mind, I find the path that leads only to Thomael. "Are we safe? Can I nurse our sons?"

His head nods, almost imperceptibly, and I lift my blouse to expose a breast. No one pays any attention to what I am doing. "Lanon, please."

My first son is lain in my arms carefully and I pull him to feed.

"Leeiss, please." I say to Jerren and Kinim. Janele has recommended I alternate first feedings with my sons to ensure they are nourished correctly. Joeve and Leeiss had the last first feeding. At the next, Joeve and Lanon will be first.

Jerren lays his son in my arms, while Kinim slides my blouse up enough for Leeiss to latch on.

"Thank you both."

They both nod their heads the same way Thomael did and go back to watching the street. Joeve is such a good baby, waiting his turn to eat. I watch Kinim sit down on the bench by the Elorcuian, and speak lovingly to his son. The Elorcuian smiles at them and continues eating.

Thomael takes a seat beside me. He wraps an arm around my shoulder and pulls me close.

"Are there many families like ours on Elorcui?" I ask Jerren in my mind.

It amazes me how much we don't speak out loud anymore. We don't really need to, but choose to do so frequently.

"Not many, min eurozan. Almost all families are male and female. To have Mated Becomings is rare."

There is that word again, rare.

"I don't realize how truly special you all are." I think as Leeiss and Lanon finish eating. They have fallen asleep. Their fathers take them and I begin feeding Joeve. "I mean, I know you are all special to me, but why don't Elorcuians see us as an anomaly?"

"Our scents." Thomael answers. "They smell all of us on you and know that we love one another. They see the love on all of our faces. They do not concern themselves with who is in the relationship, as long as there is love."

"And we have that in abundance for you." Kinim glances lovingly at his son. "And for our sons."

"All the other details do not matter to them." Jerren speaks telepathically.

He's left something unsaid. I am sure of it. Many of the Elorcuians glance or stare respectfully at my most recent Mate as we passed. Some even bow or curtsy slightly. It is odd to see such an Earthly custom be displayed by these people.

"Do not concern yourself with how they treat Jerren." Joeve is sleeping and Kinim takes him from my arms, but doesn't continue speaking.

For now, I dismiss how those of Elorcui observe my Mate. Instead I focus on the vendors before me.

"Have you changed your mind on wanting anything?" Jerren asks, as we stand as one.

I adjust my clothing and reach for the harness. "No, thank you." Not until I can bring something of my own to barter.

"I think we are fine to carry our sons back, min eurozan." Kinim says, looking to Thomael.

Thomael hands Lanon to me and takes the carrier to throw over his shoulder. "Yes. We will be fine to walk back together."

We begin our trek back to the flying machine. "It's all so beautiful here. So much to see and hear and smell and do." I watch a man, at what I would think is a pottery wheel. He's creating a large vessel. "I would still love to set up like these people and try to get others to purchase what I sell. Then I can be contributing to society too."

"One step at a time, min eurozan," Jerren says, drawing

his arm through mine.

Kinim moves to my side as we walk and Thomael walks directly behind us.

"You must first get through today, before we even discuss the possibility." Kinim states. "You are doing beautifully. I knew you would."

"Always with the flowery words, K." Thomael goads Kinim.

My Mates exchange glances.

"I hate being called K." Kinim rejoins.

"I know you do." Thomael laughs loudly in my mind.

Kinim rolls his eyes.

As we begin to exit the area, I stop and turn my head.

"What is it, Judin?" Thomael questions.

My Mates are on alert, scanning the area with their minds and eyes. Their movements are subtle, but I notice the change in them. The children are aware of their surroundings too. Ready to be obedient to their fathers' wishes.

Their eyes follow mine to an empty area just inside the row. "There." I slide my arm out of Jerren's. "Right there." I point, but don't speak out loud.

Three heads turn to the spot, as I drop my hand.

All eyes turn to me now.

"I envision our sons, in all their ages, playing around my place in the row. I have my artwork: paintings, drawings, and models on display for all to see. People pass by, admiring my work, some even barter for what they want. I am productive and helping our family." I turn to my Mates, watching me now. They are all staring at me. "Don't you see it?"

Jerren withdraws his arm and touches my face. "We see what you see, Judin. That and so much more. One day, you will have a place here. And all will admire the beauty you create. Our children will see their mother doing what she loves." His voice takes on a hardness. "It will all come to pass, just as you have seen it."

My other two Mates nod their heads at the same time

Jerren does. They are almost too in sync sometimes.

"Let's get everyone home." Kinim states, as Jerren walks up to the door of the machine. It opens and we walk inside. As Thomael steps in last, the door shuts and we begin our journey home.

"Did you have a good time?" Jerren lays Leeiss down in one of the baby cribs and moves over to me.

Thomael takes Lanon from my arms to hold his son.

"I did." I get to take my love in my arms and kiss him sweetly. "Thank you for today." When I lay my head on his chest, I hear his heartbeat sure and sound. Why do I not lay my head here? I see now why he does. It is nice.

"Don't we get a thank you?" Thomael says, laying our son in the crib by his brother. He takes my hand in his and tugs me from Jerren's arms.

I fall into him and smile happily. "You always get whatever you want, T, and you know it." I wink to him.

He scoffs. "T." He leans down to capture my lips with his and I am kissed soundly. "You are right, I do get what I want." I am let go of as he swats me playfully on the behind.

"Hey." I yelp, excitedly, glaring at him.

"I'm glad you enjoyed your big day." Kinim stands off to the side, watching all of the activity around him. He's already placed Joeve in the crib beside his brothers.

"I did, Kinim. Thank you."

He steps over to me but doesn't bring me close. Instead, he watches me. "The carrier is beautifully constructed and sturdy. It holds our sons well. Your artwork will be just as magnificent."

"You can see that?" I ask, shy that he would speak of what I have yet to create.

"I see you making artwork and so much more, min eurozan. You will do whatever you set your mind to." There is a slight frown to his countenance when he says that.

"What?" I question, moving closer to him. "You got all sad there for a moment. Why?" The thought of my Mate sad quiets my heart a little. I never want to see him troubled.

I bring my arms around him. His come around me, holding me close. "You are strong, Judin. Probably the strongest of all of us. And you are a survivor. No matter what comes at you, you meet it head on and use it to make you better. You always will."

"Don't." I say, laying my head on his solid chest. Here, I am home, and I never want to leave it. "We've had a good time in the city. Don't cast a pall over our happiness." I look up to him and he smiles sweetly at me.

"You are my first love, min eurozan, and you will be my last. My forever begins and ends with you."

"And mine with you." I remark, bringing my lips to his. Our kiss is tender and we linger in our love.

Jerren clears his throat and I turn in Kinim's arms to glance at my Mate. "We are home."

Home. The only place I ever want to be. With the best Mates a woman could ever ask for. And the most wonderful boys a mother can ever want.

My world is them, and I want nothing to change that. Ever.

CHAPTER FIFTEEN
A Deeper Connection

"*M*in eurozan." Kinim says aloud, as he bolts up in our bed.

It's the middle of the night and we are all suddenly on full alert.

My other two Mates move to shield me from danger while glancing to the screens. Our sons are sleeping peacefully. Thomael and Jerren, at the same time, look me over.

"I'm fine." I tell them, also looking at the screens to our sons.

When they are satisfied, they glance to Kinim.

"What is it?" Jerren asks telepathically, sweeping me up in his arms. It's a protective measure meant to keep me safe.

Thomael moves in front of us, ready to tear whatever is threatening me apart. Adrenaline pours through his veins like molten lava.

I feel its rush, just like it's happening in my own body. Kinim's apprehension, and Jerren's quiet curiosity also crowds my mind.

"Something is happening within your body." Kinim answers, almost tearing me from Jerren's arms. I am sat upright, as he brings his fingertips to my head.

"What are you doing?"

His eyes close as the tips of his fingers search my naked body. The movements aren't seductive or sensual, but inquisitive.

"What is Kinim doing? Jerren? Thomael?" I look to my other Mates, questioningly.

Thomael glances to Jerren.

Jerren turns to us. "When I was him, I travelled with some healers for several years. I was trained in how to read the body's changing energy. When the healers decided to stop travelling with me, I had become proficient in the practice."

Kinim's fingertips continue swirling on my body.

"I was with Kinim for five years. We never travelled with any people like that."

Jerren smiles thoughtfully at me. "When I left you as Thomael, I spent nine hundred and ninety-five years travelling the universe. It wasn't until I was at the end of my life that I came back for you in the circle."

"That's impossible. You weren't gone that long," I reply. "It is a while, yes, but not that long."

Kinim withdraws his fingertips from me and moves back on our bed. "Yes, I was."

I turn to him, curious now. "What is it? What did you find? And what do you mean, 'Yes, I was?'"

He reaches forward to draw me into his arms again. The move is a careful one. "You will be starting your cycle again very soon. You are not with child."

"Oh." I bring my hands together in my lap. "You can sense that?"

"As our time together passes, we are all becoming better at reading one another. We sense your thoughts and moods. Also, changes in your habits and personality." Jerren eyes Kinim and then myself. "Kinim, more than I can sense your body's changes as it occurs."

"Why can't you?" I ask Jerren. "You are Kinim."

"I'm over a thousand years older than the Mate that holds you in his arms. I've lived longer than he and have acquired a vast amount of knowledge Kinim can not possess." Jerren replies, patiently.

"We all have strengths and attributes that help our family, min eurozan." Thomael says, as his hands bring me to our bed. He lays me down flat and nestles my center. "It strengthens us and makes our, what you call a family, complete."

Jerren curls up to my left side and lays his head on my chest. His favorite spot.

Kinim spoons me from my right. He brings an arm around my neck, as I melt into him.

Drifting off to sleep, a thought occurs to me. "What are we, if not a family?"

Jerren tilts his head up to look into my eyes. "You call us a family, but we are more than that. All through time and space, your Mates are One. We have not always been, but shall be as long as we have you to live for."

Kimin's fingertips touch my cheek, comforting my thoughts.

"And our sons?" I ask, wondering what will become of them, after our brightly lit stars have burned out and cease to be more.

Jerren continues speaking. "Our children and their children will shine on for us. Their love and spirit will show others our love for many eons to come." His gaze softens, as he watches me. "Shall I put you to sleep to rest, min eurozan?"

"No, my love," I say, as my Mates draw close to me. "I'm a big girl and can do it myself."

Thomael chuckles quietly.

Kinim withdraws the tips of his fingers from my cheek. His kiss to the top of my head is light. "Sleep well, Judin."

I'm already falling into the same dream I always have of them. They welcome me with open arms into the vastness of their world and into time without end. "I love you all."

***

A light kiss rouses me from my slumber. His lower lip rounded and smooth. The upper lip is thin, his moustache tickles me.

"Jerren," I sigh, bringing my hands to his neck as he deepens the kiss.

A finely chiseled hand comes to my right breast and begins kneading gently. His thumb plays over the top of my globe, as I arch to meet it.

I reach for the owner of that hand with my mind and breathe out his name. "Kinim."

"Min eurozan." His response is just as wanting and rich, as he continues caressing me.

In the very center of my body I begin to feel a warm wetness. Thomael's tongue has come into play, sliding up to my navel, as he dives in to draw me into him.

My senses go into overdrive.

Thomael comes back to my center, slowly beginning to build the fire.

Jerren's other hand caresses my globe close to him. His motions are unlike Kinim's. They are careful, yet conveying the want he has.

"Jerren wants you, min eurozan." Kinim whispers into my ear. "Will you let him have you?"

My Mates have never taken me against my will. No matter who I was with, I am more than adequately prepared for the physical part of our loving, well before it begins. Before it was over, we all are truly satisfied.

I want to weep at the pleasure my Mates are giving me. If there is some way to repay them for the love they have for me, I would gladly do so. Without hesitation.

"Yes." I say, bringing up a hand and running my fingertips over Jerren's cheek. My other hand is in Kinim's hair, stroking it in the way he loves.

The very core of my being begins to throb under Thomael's ministrations.

"I want you on the edge of ecstasy, before we become one, min eurozan. I want to feel your sweetness pounding against me when I enter you. Then I want to show you the stars as we soar, becoming one."

The throbbing becomes insistent as Thomael eagerly continues his most luscious activity. Just as I feel myself on the precipice, Thomael moves from me.

"We have a treat for you." Jerren says, as Thomael and Kinim move me.

My head now almost completely lies over the side of our bed and Kinim stands in front of me. Thomael straddles my waist. Jerren pushes my legs up, as he positions himself at my entrance.

"You have been quite eager to taste me." Kinim says, bringing himself close. "Here I am now. Satisfy your curiosity." I open my mouth to receive him.

"And I want you to receive my essence." Thomael whispers seductively into my mind, as he brings my breast together and inserts himself between them. "So perfect."

"And you shall carry me in your womb throughout the day." Jerren slowly begins entering into my body. When he is seated, there is a cessation in movements. Each focus on the feel of what is happening within themselves, and with me.

My Mates' voices focus on me. The sensation of having the three of them where they are is heady.

"I love you, min eurozan." The unity of their voices almost send me tumbling off the edge, but I regain control.

"And I love you." I speak to them in my mind, lovingly.

As the last syllable slips from my mind, my Mates begin moving. Each of their thoughts only on what is happening between the two of us.

Jerren is more than enjoying the feel of entering and exiting my body, finding the one spot that is making me writhe on the bed.

Thomael's hands and thoughts become about how to please me and how he feels sliding between the rounds on my chest.

Kinim luxuriates in the enjoyment he is finding in my mouth, careful to make sure that I am delighted to receive his joy.

Our lovemaking continues and my Mates show me stars, like Jerren has promised many times.

Jerren abandons himself to the pleasures he finds within my core, not withdrawing when he is spent, but holding me close.

Thomael comes to end of himself, his essence on my stomach, and lays himself next to my hip.

Kinim's fingertips hold my cheeks where he wants, as he loses himself to the decadence surrounding him.

We are sweaty, hot, and utterly satisfied, as they withdraw and lie down on the bed. Each of my Mates move to take their customary sleeping position. Our scents blend to create a new one and I revel in having a part of my Mates inside and on me. Our love may not be accepted on Earth, like it is on Elorcui, but our ties tare deeper and longer lasting.

Exhaustion begins to overtake us all. Once again, I am wrapped up in their love. Contentment flows through their thoughts as they begin to drift into sleep. I glance to the screens and notice our sons are smiling too. Their grins matching that of their fathers. I wonder if they feel the pure happiness in our minds, as they slumber.

"Sleep." The command is pushed into my mind from each of my Mates. I fall into the sweet, dark abyss of their unending love.

***

When I awake, the bed is empty except for myself. I look to the screens and see our sons aren't in their cribs.

"We are caring for them." Kinim speaks into my thoughts, reassuring me. "Jerren has already gone for the day."

"Our son is with his father and we are content. We

thought you might enjoy the rest." Thomael projects an image of the five of them outside in the sunsshine. "If you wish, sleep longer and when our son is hungry, we will wake you."

I bring all of their pillows close to me and breathe in their scents. My Mates are so good to me!

A burst of energy shoots through me and I slip from the bed. I should dress for the day, but don't want to do so. It was suggested I could walk through the house without any clothing on, if our sons are sleeping, but I want to feel the air on my skin.

Better yet, the suns on it. Yes!

The house is surrounded by lots of green grass with no neighbors for miles around. I open the doors to our balcony and peek outside. My Mates and our sons are nowhere to be seen. I do see the individual trees, as if I am standing in front of them.

I fling open the doors and walk proudly out into the sunsslight. My pores 'open' and I feel them draw in what is offered by the rays. A feeling of warmth and light enters my being. I can't help to smile!

There is a wooden railing that runs around the balcony. I bring my hands to it, feeling its heat, and bringing it into myself.

As I lift my face to the suns, the sensation is like nothing I have ever experienced.

I hear a slight chuckle behind me and turn to see Thomael and Kinim watching me.

"I see you have taken Jerren's suggestion and have chosen to walk around for us to see." Thomael calls, as his eyes take in my form.

"I wanted to feel the sunsslight on me." I reply, looking into his eyes.

"And?" His eyes hold mine now.

"It feels delicious." I say, smiling at my Mates.

"You think many things are delicious," Thomael shoots

back, "but only one thing really hits the spot." His wink is quick.

"Every time." I smile back, catching Kinim's eye.

"We have decided, once you have breakfast and fed our sons, that we would take another trip to the market." Thomael exclaims.

"Really?" I'm already planning what I will wear and do. "What did Jerren say? Did he approve?"

"It is his idea. He wants you Marked with our essence and our sons with you as before. He says he will oversee our visit." Thomael answers.

I feel their eyes on me as I walk to our closet. They are my Mates and while I feel their appreciation of my form, they are eager to begin the day, too. "I wanted to see Jerren off…"

Kinim chuckles quietly, and I turn to look at him.

Thomael smirks knowingly. "You seen him off quite well during the night."

I pick up a soft shoe and throw it at him. "You!" A giggle erupts from my throat, as I turn to Kinim. "Is that why we made love last night? To have your Scents with me today?"

"We had already made plans to take you to the market today, yes. Those plans were made before we went to bed last night. The lovemaking was an added bonus. We had planned on adding our Scents to you individually." Kinim answers.

"You were enjoying yourself quite a bit, Judin." Thomael says, striding across the room to the door. "You can't deny that."

"I don't deny it." I can't help but blush. The intense feelings of being with my Mates in such a way is a rush. If asked, I would gladly do it again.

Kinim's hands comes to my shoulders. "We want to make sure you are kept safe, min eurozan. If there comes a time when we feel it is safe for you to take our sons to the market with your art, we want to do all that we can to ensure you are one of us."

"So, it wasn't just about the crazy good time we had?" I

tease him, and Thomael.

Thomael's grin is wide, and his thoughts become how he has pleasured the two us. "Crazy good time doesn't even comes close, Judin." He straightens and catches Kinim's eye. "Our son is about ready to eat. When you and Kirim are ready, we will meet you downstairs for breakfast." The door shuts loudly behind him. He isn't happy about leaving me with my other Mate.

Upon entering the closet, I wrinkle my nose. "Uh, Kinim, why do each of your Scents linger so heavily in the air?" I ask, turning to him. It's as if my Mates are standing in my closet.

"Your senses are heightening." He replies, entering, to stand close to me. "As your Mates, we've done nothing different in this room to be more pronounced than our presence is to you." His arms come around me, pulling me close. "We are both in and on you." His kiss is tender, leaving me wanting more. "My essence lingers in your mouth. You will eat and drink this morning, but anyone within a certain distance from you will know you are mine when you exhale."

Oh. "And is the same with Thomael and Jerren's essence too?" Just before I went under, I remembered taking Thomael's essence and rubbing it into my skin.

His hands drop to my hips, urging my body to turn. My back is flush to his front. He snakes one of his arms wrapping it around my waist, as he leans close. "As your Mates, we only concentrate on having our Scent with you. When we are with you, our only thought is of you and ourselves. Because Thomael and Jerren and I are One, we lock minds to heighten your pleasure, but never discuss what you do for us." Together, he moves us over to the floor length mirror of the closet. "If you wish to know if I can Scent Thomael and Jerren in and on you, then the answer is yes."

I see his hand come to my hair and delve into it. "My Scent is in your hair and on your face from our time together last night." His fingertips drop to my neck as he speaks. "On your neck and chest is Thomael. When he completed himself on you, you rubbed him into other parts of your body, not just your chest."

I didn't realize Kinim could Scent where I has spread Thomael's Essence.

"Oh, yes." His fingertips grazes my chest and down to hover over my core. "As Thomael started your body singing, his smell lingers here, but it is Jerren's essence that anyone will scent. He will be inside you as we move through the marketplace." His touch is light, reverent. "This is where we all want to be, because your Essence strongly emanates from here."

There is a certain emotion to his voice as he speaks.

"Now that you have touched me there, your smell will linger too." I meet his eyes in the mirror.

His smile is radiant. "We are your Mates. We are One. If one of us is with you, we all are. I can't envy your moments with Thomael or Jerren, as they are my moments too. I remember myself as Thomael with you, and Jerren often allows me in his mind, when you are with him."

"Why?" I ask, cautiously.

"Because he wants me to see how you respond to him. If he does something with you that we don't do and it brings you happiness, or pain, he wants me to know, so I may use that knowledge in the future." He sighs. "You don't think of me or Thomael when you are with Jerren. As you shouldn't, so your mind is closed to us."

I turn back into his arms.

"We want to know how to bring you the most pleasure possible when we lie with you."

"So you share information? Even though I make love differently with each of you?" I ask, tentatively.

"You are our life, min eurozan. If we can give you a fraction of the joy you give us, then we are complete." He takes my hands and brings them between us. "I have to be honest with you about something. Last night, when we partook of your body, it was not only to ready you for the day, but to satisfy a need we had for you. Your pheromones are exceptionally potent right now, as you are close to your cycle. Our bodies crave you like the food we need to eat and the life giving water that refreshes our bodies."

"Do you still crave me now?" As much as I want to be with Kinim, I can't. I am too sore from last night. The memories of my Mates make me smile though.

"There will never be a time that we will not crave you. Your touch, your heart, your mind, and your soul are ours. Because you have gifted all of these things to us, we can only show you love and support."

In this moment, Kinim is the perfect Mate for me. "I only return the love that is given to me." I say, drawing closer to him.

"That is your heart talking. I am your heart. When you are with Thomael, your body speaks volumes. When Jerren is around, he sparks your soul."

A thought flits through my mind of Jaed.

"He will always be your mind. Your intellect shines when you think of him with us. The four of us make the one man you need. Always." Kinim coos, happily. "But right now, our sons need the nourishment that only their mother can give them." He walks over to select a sundress that buttons down the front to the waist. "This will do nicely, as we move through the streets. Our Scents will radiate from your skin and will allow for our sons to be fed, should they become hungry. Plus," he says, handing me the dress, "you will look beautiful in it."

"Do you really think so, Kinim?" I despise dresses.

"You would look beautiful covered in ashes and your hair blowing wildly in the wind." He replies, stepping back across the room. "Please, do hurry. Our sons are becoming rather insistent with Thomael." His chuckle is low, as he shuts the door behind himself.

I don the dress quickly. If my Mate thinks I will look beautiful in a dress, then I will wear it for him, and Thomael.

They are of one mind when it comes to me, so my other Mate should love it too.

CHAPTER SIXTEEN
The Day Out

*a*s soon as my feet touch the bottom step, Thomael whisks me up in his arms. "There you are." He says, kissing me soundly, while carrying me to the breakfast room. As I am set in my seat, he smiles widely at me. "When Kinim said he selected this dress for you, he said that it you would look exquisite in it, he was right."

Kinim is already picking up Joeve and Leeiss to breakfast with us. We settle the two into eating, as my Mate begins preparing my breakfast plate.

Thomael scoops up his son and sits back down at the table.

"I'm eager to begin the trip today. I know exactly where I would love to have my space and sell my art. I've been picturing when I would set up my paintings and other works. The children will be beside me the whole time, of course, and I will be near the vessel that can take me home quickly."

"You have been thinking." Thomael moves to pile food onto his plate. Once he is done, he sets it in front of him and begins eating one-handed. "I like that."

"We shall have to find out how our excursions go first, Judin. We had no issues the first time, but that was with Jerren. He will be overseeing today, but not with us." Kinim says, cautiously.

"Except..." I glance down to my lap.

"Yes." Thomael huffs. "We made sure you are Marked well with our Scents. Even now, I sense Jerren with us."

He would know. That particular area of my body is his favorite spot. "Don't worry, my Mate, you shall reclaim your prize again soon."

Thomael's smile is quick, prideful.

Joeve and Leeiss finish eating and Kinim takes them from my arms. Thomael lays Lanon close to my breast and our son begins eating heartily.

Thomael resumes eating his breakfast.

I pick up my fork and begin eating too. It still amazes me how many Earth-like everyday items are being utilized in Elorcui.

"So, how is this going to go down?" I ask, after I swallow my bite. "We are leaving after breakfast so that we can make it a full day, right? I want to get the feel of the market. See who is selling what and how transactions are done. I want to introduce myself to others too." I'm famished, and begin eating quickly, as Lanon greedily nurses at my breast.

"One step at a time," Thomael cautions. "First we see how everyone reacts when it is just the two of us. If all is well, we will allow you take our sons to the market. We will already be there, at a distance, when you and our sons arrive. If all goes well then too, we will discuss another visit without us."

Kinim throws Thomael a dangerous look.

"From a distance, K. Our Mate wants freedom, and we will give it to her. If we deem it safe."

"You know what can happen if they get their hands on Judin." Kinim states flatly. He's angry, and I don't know why.

"If who gets their hands on me?" I ask, swiveling my head back and forth between my Mates.

"Yes, I do, and I would tear this world apart to have her back with us." Thomael declares violently, surprising me.

Unlike Thomael, Kinim's extremely violent streak is well

hidden under layers of love, affection, and humor.

When Thomael makes something – or someone – his, he gives them everything he is. Heaven help anyone who takes what is his.

Not long after I had start travelling through time and space with Thomael, I was mistaken for some civilization's goddess. In their custom, once she appeared, she is to be lavished with gifts, rich food, and then sacrificed.

Thomael found out where I was, what was happening, and was not happy.

There had been much discussion as to whether I should stay a hostage or allowed to be freed. Infighting began that escalated into a full scale planetary war.

Thomael found a way into where I was being held and freed me. Carnage was everywhere. He kept walking through it all, dragging me behind him, until he found a particular spot. He said nothing to try to quell the rage happening around us. I had seen Thomael bring peace to entire planets with just a few well-timed words. These people were not so lucky. A coldness masked his eyes, as he watched all of the atrocities around them. Those dark eyes turned to me, he pulled me close, and then we were gone.

Thomael vowed to never return to the planet again. Later in our wanderings, we had heard that their entire population was decimated by a thermonuclear device that had killed everyone on the entire planet. Thomael smirked coldly and we never spoke of it again.

"Those living outside the city. They don't follow our rules," I say, remembering what I was told by my Mates. "You are both worried about what will happen if myself, or our sons are captured."

Kinim's hand shoots out to hold mine. "Nothing would happen to our sons, min eurozan. They would be raised by someone of our city. But they would burn you alive and announce that they have killed a visitor. It would start a planet wide search for others like you."

Thomael's fist slams down on the table, making me jump. "Had to tell her that, did you, K?"

"Are there? Others, like me?" I ask, after recovering from Thomael's outburst.

"No, Judin. There have not been visitors since the citizens of this world agreed we would let no one on this planet." Kinim comes to his knees beside my chair. "But your body chemistry is changing, and you are our Mate." His eyes find Thomael's. "Jerren's Mate."

Something is left unsaid. I was sure of it. "I don't want to know the specifics, but Jerren is a man of importance. My death as his Mate - your Mate," I glance from Kinim to Thomael and then back. "Being Jerren's Mate wouldn't save me, and still risk all of your lives?"

"Yes." Thomael grounds out. "Even with Jerren's position in our government, you might not be saved. Questions would be asked that demanded answers."

"This is why you are kept here, min eurozan. Your body is transitioning to be more like ours. Your sense of smell has already sharpened. With every passing day, I scent less of Earth from you. Here, you are kept safe and we get to live a life with you." Kinim's words are sweet. But I hear the danger in them.

"If I am found out, I will be killed." My mind fills in the gaps. "Rather publicly, and it will put you all in danger?"

"Yes." Thomael offers again.

I push my plate away. Had I realized I was putting my family in such danger, I wouldn't have insisted on going to the city. I would have found a way to coexist with my Mates and our sons, without being such a burden. At least until I am more like my Mates and our sons.

A single tear slides down my cheek, and I bury my head in my hands. "I'm so sorry."

I hear the sounds of chairs scraping the wooden floor and two sets of arms pulling me close.

"Judin, please don't cry. There's no need." Kinim. My

heart. "We do not mean to frighten you, but want you to know what path we are already headed down together."

"I'll be killed?" I ask, pulling out of their arms. "Have you seen that?" I turn to Thomael and then back to Kinim. "Have you three seen my death?"

They exchange glances. It's Thomael who speaks. "No, min eurozan. You will not die by the hands of those who live outside Elorcui. Truth be told, we have not seen your death. I Become K and K Becomes Jaad and Jaad Became Jerren. But you live on."

There's more. Again. "What?"

"The future before us is already in motion." Thomael's words echo Jerren's. "We continue with our plans."

"What's going to happen?" I look to my Mates, who exchange glances again. "Tell me. What's going to happen to our sons? To me?"

"We don't know." Kinim says. "But you will be kept safe and protected. Our sons will be kept secure."

I stand now, and move away from them. Resolve motivates me now. "If our future is already set into motion and we are slaves to its will, then I say we meet it. Kick it in its teeth and show it who the boss really is." I fist my hands at my sides. It's my turn to make a Thomael move. "If I have to be Scented again from both of you in any way, do it. If I need to be Marked... or branded... or whatever, do it. I'll die a thousand deaths to keep my Mates and our sons safe."

Both of my Mates peer up at me from the floor in awe.

Thomael's fists come to his sides and shake a little.

Kinim looks ready to supplicate himself at my feet.

They both stand at the same time and make their way over to where I am standing. Thomael stops directly in front of me, and Kinim is at my back.

"Our warrior queen," Thomael says, pinching a strand of my hair between his fingers. "You are fierce and tough when you need to be. Soft and yielding when being taken. You are the universe's perfect gift to us."

One of Kinim's hands rest on my hip. The fingertips of his other hand begins stroking my cheek. "You shall burn like the brightest star, and be our center. We shall move around you and decimate worlds in your name. And you shall love us more with every passing eon."

His hand cups my chin and turns my head towards him. Our lips meet and stars dance behind my eyelids.

Thomael wraps his hand in my hair and pulls me from Kinim. "Mine." His lips bruise mine, in a kiss that would set worlds on fire.

***

As the flight to the marketplace begins, we are all silent. I want the trip to be one filled with hope and promise. It is, but now it is so much more. Our future as a family, as a whole unit, is on the line, and I am going to do everything in my power to make sure we do all we can to meet it head on.

After the children have eaten breakfast, I ask Kinim to watch our sons, while I invite Thomael back to our bedroom. Before he stumbles from our room, wide smile on his face, I am marked with his Scent once again.

In my mind, I call Kinim next. It is Thomael's turn to watch our sons while Kinim's scent is reapplied. Kinim's smile is happy, as he exits our room to ready our sons for the day.

Back in our bedroom closet, I walk to Jerren's side and select one of his button down shirts. My chest is bigger than his, so I wear it over the dress Kinim has picked out. Between being Scented twice by two of my Mates, and Jerren's scent in my core and on his shirt, along with Thomael, Kinim, and our sons releasing their scents, when we step out of the flying machine, I know my scent as an Earthling will be well covered.

Our sons sense the change in our attitudes and intentions.

Lanon's gaze finds his father's, and I know they are speaking to one another without me.

Kinim holds Joeve in one arm during the entire flight,

while holding my other hand. Occasionally, Kinim's eyes would flick to Joeve, and I would notice a nod or shake of the head. Again, almost imperceptible, but they were speaking.

Leeiss slept securely in my other arm. His words are filled with love and peace. He is so much like his father and I adore our son more, for having Jerren's calm demeanor.

I need Leeiss's reassurance. On the outside, I try to project a demeanor of resolve and firm conviction. On the inside, I am afraid. My family is everything and I don't want to lose what we are building.

But fate is trying it's best to tear us apart, and that worried me. What if, because of my selfishness, I have put us all in danger? What if I am found out and my Mates pay the price for keeping me? Maybe we should abort the idea of the marketplace and I ask to be brought back to Earth, without Lanon, Joeve, and Leeiss. There are women who can nurture our sons with their milk. And it would take our family out of the danger we are in. No matter how my heart would feel, bleeding and broken, I will do what I need to do. For them.

Thomael growls, flashing his blue eyes at me. "No. You don't leave us. Ever."

Kinim squeezes my hand, reassuringly. "We can read your thoughts, min eurozan. Everything you think is known to us." He leans over to touch my cheek. "No matter what course we decide on, the universe already has us where we need to be. Trust in it, and your Mates."

I speak now only to Kinim. "But what if I am found out? I don't fear for my life, but for our sons and my Mates. I would gladly die a thousand deaths, rather than allow any of you to suffer because of me."

"When we made love to you, we set this course into motion. You are our past, present, and future. Nothing will ever change that. Not for you, or for us." There is a certain resolve in his voice, and something else.

"What is it, Kinim?" I ask, holding his hand tighter.

Thomael moves his eyes back and forth between us. He

can hear Kinim's thoughts, but not mine.

"You doubt us, Judin. We may not see everything, but we see ourselves with you and forever. There is a lot we can't see, but we do see that. If you can't trust in us, trust in that." Kinim is hurt and I am the one who hurt him.

I fall to my knees, carefully as Leeiss is in my arms, and lay my head on his knee. When next I speak, it is out loud. "I do trust in my Mates. I do. It is the future I am afraid of, my love."

A hand drops softly on my shoulder. It's Thomael's. I would know his touch anywhere. "We are your future, min eurozan. Nothing else matters."

I bring one of my hands to cover his. "You're right." I lift my head to peer at Kinim. "You're both right. I want my forever to love you all. It's not so much to ask."

Thomael brings his hand to grasp mine. "You will have it, min eurozan." His words are like those etched in stone. They can't be unwritten, and his resolve won't be shaken. Come Hell or high water, he will give me what I want. What he wants.

Kinim touches my cheek. "We are here."

As I stand, Thomael's hand slips from mine and Kinim drops his hand. "It's time for me to carry our sons through the streets." I hand Leeiss to Kinim and slip on the harness. My Mates begin adding their sons. Lanon in front, Joeve on my hip, and Leeiss on my back. "They're getting heavier."

"Your cycle is soon. I feel the tiredness in your body and the ache settling into your limbs." Kinim glances to Thomael and back to me. My other Mate nods his head. "When you are ready to leave, let us know." Kinim is using his Thomael voice. "We will return and go home immediately."

"Yes, sir." I carefully salute, badly, and turn to Thomael. "Anything else?"

His lips touch mine, softly. "Just love us." Thomael's voice, but I hear Kinim.

"Forever." I whisper, glancing from one Mate to the other, as I think the words to Jerren.

"I am here, Judin." Jerren says, slightly distracted. "My meeting is finishing and I shall oversee your outing from where I am."

"I hope it went well, min eurozan. I love you." Happiness is beamed to me like sunsshine, and I feel blessed. "Well, let's go."

Kinim moves to the door and it opens. The sunslight floods the entrance and we move toward it. Thomael is the first out the door, I am second with our sons, and as Kinim exits, the door closes behind us. My Mates flank me, and I "see" what looks like spores releasing from a mushroom, leaving their bodies and wrapping around mire. I've never actually seen them do anything like this before.

I smile, and think to my Mates. "I think I just seen your Scents."

Thomael's smile widens.

"Your eyesight is improving." Kinim responds to my statement.

"Can they see that?" I ask, watching those in the marketplace before us.

"No." Thomael begins moving and I follow. Kinim is with us as we walk. "Only those who move through time and space like us can see it. To my knowledge, we are the only ones who can do so, at will."

"Oh." I say, noting the first stall at the marketplace.

"Is that why Jerren has the position he does?" I ask, willing myself not to glance at the tallest building in town, where I was kept for months, waiting for my Mates. "Because you can all travel that way, if you choose?"

Kinim eyes a piece of bright red fabric and glances to me. I have never seen a weave like it before. "Yes. As Jerren is us in this time, he is the one in charge."

Thomael shakes his head, almost imperceptibly.

"What?" I ask Thomael, as he ushers us on.

"The less you know about your Mate's position in Elorcui, Judin, the better." Thomael moves ahead of us, just a little.

"Why?" I ask, digging my heels into the soft brown "dirt". It looks like dirt, but the consistency isn't the same. It's a mix of hard ground and sand.

Thomael comes back to us and takes my arm, politely. "The information would only bring you harm in the future."

In the future. I stumble, and then move on with him. "I shouldn't know that then."

His glittering blue eyes find mine. They are hard. "No, you shouldn't."

Okay. Then I won't know anything, I muse, and continue on with my Mates and our sons.

I begin to note the people of Elorcui. They are like those on Earth, all shapes and sizes. The only difference is that their coloring isn't the same. They are all a light tan, almost like a splash of creamer in my morning coffee on Earth.

My Mates, our sons, and I must stick out like a sore thumb.

"You are Jerren's Mate," Kinim offers, "and we are his Becomings. While we are of this world, we have been affected by our adventures. We don't look like those of our world anymore."

"You're anomalies? Like I am." I say, continuing to walk with my Mates. "And because of Jerren's position in the city, we are accepted."

The nod of Kinim's head is slight.

I note a seller who has a small child, no more than two. He's beautiful looking. His gaze is downcast and his hair is dirty. A thick layer of dust covers his skin.

"Would you like a pomman, Haulto Un?" She offers. In her hand is what looks to be a cross between an apple and a pear.

"Should I?" I ask Thomael.

"You must give her something in return."

I have nothing on me, so I shake my head, declining her offer.

"I give this to you freely, Haulto Un," she insists, bowing

slightly. "Please accept this gift."

Kinim smiles, as he takes it from her hand. "On behalf of Haulto Un, thank you." He withdraws what looks to be new pencil from his shirt pocket. It doesn't look like any writing utensil I have ever seen before, but I see what looks like lead inside the wood. "For you." He glances toward her child. "For help in selling your wares. From Haulto Un."

She bows slightly and I see her cheeks stain blue. Not red, but blue. I school my face not to react.

"You are very generous, Haulto Un. Remgra."

I take a moment to digest the word and say it is my mind.

"Very good, Judin." This from Kinim, my encourager.

Thomael nods his head at me.

Again, I take a moment and think the words Kinim said to my mind.

Kinim looks to Thomael who nods his head. "Now tell her, de rien."

My eyes meet hers and they are grey, like flint. They're beautiful. I catch myself staring at them. "De rien." I repeat the words out loud, as I have pronounced them in my mind.

She smiles slightly, and steps back into her stall.

Thomael ushers us on. "Very good, min eurozan."

The compliment surprises me, as it was not Kinim who said it, but Thomael.

"De rien." I repeat, smiling slightly. "What does 'Haulto Un' mean?"

Thomael and Kinim exchange quick glances, but don't answer my question.

This perturbs me until the words from earlier come back to me. "I should know."

"We will only tell you what you must know, Judin." Thomael's protective nature is making its presence known.

It irritates me to know they don't tell me things, because they think it will keep me safe. But I have our sons to consider, so I hold my tongue.

I glance around and note everyone has the same eye

color. My Mates do not have that particular esthetic. It must be because of their genetic rarity. Our sons have their father's colorings and their eye color. They, too, are a genetic outcast.

"Do the people of this world not see me as someone different than them?" I ask all of my Mates. "How do they not see me as a visitor?"

Thomael and Kinim exchange glances again. It is Kinim who answers the question.

"Our Scent. Those of Elorcui see what we want them to see. When you are Marked it masks what you truly look like."

"But Janele and Christan have no issue with how I look. Both have seen me without your Scentings or Markings." I muse.

"They are part of the Trusted. Those Jerren trusts to take care of his everyday life at work, and Janele is your, what you would call, caregiver. Christan only serves Jerren, and Janele only ministers to you. Both do not care if you are a visitor, especially as you are Jerren's Mate." Thomael answers, stopping at the end of the street.

"Are there many Trusted?" I ask, sitting down and beginning to remove our sons from the carrier. I feel physically drained and am ready for a rest.

"No." Kinim says, taking Joeve and then Leeiss from me.

Thomael removes Lanon and sits at my side.

I find the path only meant for Kinim. "I think Thomael is getting frustrated at me."

"It's not you, min eurozan. The universe is calling him." Kinim adds in, glancing to Thomael. "He needs to leave us."

"Now?" I ask, trying not to panic. "We just arrived." I move to stand. "Then we will go home and come again another day."

Kinim is watching Thomael. Their minds are closed to me. Thomael glances sharply to Kinim and then back to our flying vessel. His eyes find mine and his son. They come back to Kinim.

"Go." I say into Thomael's mind, making sure Kinim can

hear me.

An Elorcuian sits down on the bench away from us.

I move closer to Kinim who lays an arm on my shoulder. "If you have to leave us then do so. We will make our way back to the flying machine and then home. We will be quick and not rush, but hurry."

Kinim and Thomael continue talking, but I see the urgency in Thomael's body language. At home, he wouldn't feel rushed, but he is needing to leave.

"Go." I stand and hand Leeiss to Kinim. "I will be at home when you return. We'll celebrate our love once again." My kiss to him is lingering and I gently take Lanon from his arms. "We shall see you again soon, min eurozan."

Thomael's arm snakes around my waist and pulls me close. His dark eyes flash to Kinim. Kinim nods his head once, and Thomael releases me to hurry off.

"He loves you very much, Judin." Kinim speaks softly in my mind. "He's worried about not being here for the rest of our visit." His eyes scan the area and then rest on me.

"I know. Let's make our way back." I place Lanon in front of me and take Leeiss from Kinim. He slides Leeiss on my back and Joeve to my side. He brings my hand into his. "Let's take our time walking back. If anything is amiss, I will let you know. Make our way to the machine and it will take us home. Jerren can be here soon, if we need him."

We begin walking again. The same man sits at the "pottery wheel", churning out a new creation. His last creation is sitting in front of his space, ready to be bartered. I see what looks to be fish drying in the sun. Except, once again, the fish are nothing like I have ever seen. They are flat and wide. The bones are see through and there is plenty of meat on it.

The people are all dressed in variations of the same cream color, as I had seen in Jaad's office. The colors compliment the gold of the buildings, that slope down to provide shade to those bartering on the streets.

"Are there any restaurants or theatres in the city?" I ask,

as we walk.

"No. Food is what one can find. There is plenty on this world if one takes the time to find it. We don't have restaurants like you do on Earth, we congregate in one another's home if we wish to share food that each person brings. We do have games like what you would call chess and other amusements though. They are entertaining. Our life in Elorcui is very simple."

"Oh."

We are halfway down the street, when we pass the space where I was offered the fruit, I glance to it. The child is standing by its mother, but staring at me. His eyes, I swear, are blue. Not like Thomael's, but blue nonetheless. Upon closer inspection, I see a shot of red in his hair. Bright red. A smear of dirt on his face, belies a pale complexion.

As I turn to Kinim to remark on these things, I feel my stomach spasm and my cycle begins.

One by one each Elorcuian begins lifting their faces and lightly sniffing.

"We must get back home." Kinim says in my mind. "Your cycle has begun."

He picks up our pace, just a little and we move through the streets. "They can't sense that, can they?"

An Elorcuian turns to look our way and lifts his head. I see his nostrils flare.

Kinim stops and I see him will his Scent out of him and into the air. It bursts around me and I see it hover in the air. Our sons do the same and I am almost overwhelmed by the mix of Scents.

The Elorcuian shakes his head and turns from us.

"You all do that consciously." I remark, as we get closer to the ship. "I thought that is an unconscious gesture," I muse aloud.

"Conscious only to protect our Mate and our family." Kinim replies. As we near the machine, the door opens and he ushers us inside. As the door shuts, he takes our sons from me and sits down in one of the chairs.

"Are you alright?" I ask, squatting down to watch him.

"They all suspected something was amiss, but couldn't figure out what it was. When I saw one of them look to you, I had to do something. So I through him off of your Scent. We Scented and Marked you, yet your body overcame us." Kinim's voice is a mix of frustration and awe.

I didn't know what to say. First Thomael had to leave us and then my cycle begun. None of that was in my control.

Kinim reaches for and brings me to his lap. "I don't blame you, but I do worry for your safety. My only thought is that I had to get you off of the street." His fingertips touch my cheek. "I have told Jerren and he will be making a visit to the marketplace soon. For now, we are on the way home and all is well."

I lean back into the arms of my Mate. As much as I was ready for the day out, I am ready to be home. To be surrounded by Mates, our sons, and our home life, is more than I could ever want.

"Yes, my love. Let's go home."

Kinim's arms come around me and I fall into a light sleep, as we make our way there.

CHAPTER SEVENTEEN
The Promise

$\mathcal{T}$homael returns two days later full of energy and excitement. I am swept up in his arms as soon as he walks through the front door and receive a long, deep kiss. His nostrils flare and he growls. "As soon as your cycle has ended, I will be the first Mate to have you. I've missed you, min eurozan, and I want to love you our way."

Our way meant hair pulling and light play. I would be sore the next day and we would both be smiling.

"Well, my love," I give back to him, "I want our loving too. I want to be in charge of our loving times. You get to have all the fun." I pout, bringing him close. "I want to play, too."

"Then my body will be your playground and you shall play, until your heart is content, or I am ready to be satisfied, after you are begging for me."

Yes, please.

"Your son wants to see his father," Kinim announces, bringing Lanon over to us.

Joeve is in his other arm and my Mates stand close to me.

Their eyes clash again and I know they are speaking to one another.

The door opens and Jerren comes in from work for the

159

day.

"My love." I let go of Thomael and skip to Jerren. Our family is together again. "Thomael is home. How was your day?"

Jerren looks tired. I've never seen him so worn. "Good day, my love." His glance to Thomael is quick, knowing. They have already spoken.

"Would you like for me to get Leeiss?" Our son always cheered up his father after a stressful day. "Let me do that for you."

I turn to get our son and feel his hand on my bare arm. I would know Jerren's touch any time. "The four of us need to talk."

"Absolutely. But, I would like to get Leeiss, so that he may join his brothers." I retrieve our son from the nursery, taking him down to the family room where everyone has gathered. "Here you go. Your son." I hand him Leeiss, who smiles at his father. Jerren's face lights with happiness.

"Come, sit by me, min eurozan." Thomael calls, from the couch. Kinim is on the other side with Joeve.

I do so as Jerren and Leeiss speak to one another. I hear their words of love and joy at seeing one another again.

When they are done speaking, Jerren turns to me. "I must make a trip into the Ilestri Terrenes, the Barren Lands. I don't know how long I will be gone."

Thomael and Kinim make no reactions.

"What is the Ilestri Terrenes?" I ask, wishing I could pull one of our sons close.

Thomael's hand comes to my thigh and Kinim's arm wraps around my shoulder.

"Ilestri Terrenes is where those Elorcuians live outside the city. Their rules are not ours and they don't want to follow our ways." Jerren explains.

"Oh. How long would you be gone?" I stand now and move to him. I come to my knees before him.

"As long as necessary, min eurozan. But I will come home

to you and our son. Always." He reaches out his hand to touch my face with his fingertips.

I smile into his touch. "And I shall be waiting for you. Always. When will you be leaving?"

"A week from now. I am to meet with their Lidef a leader, or chief of the people. Those in Ilestri Terrenes follow no one, but their Lidef." Jerren continues to explain.

"If they need no one to lead them, then why do they need a Lidef?" I ponder, aloud.

"Because," he flashes a look to Thomael and Kinim, "there are times when discussions are needed. This is one of them. So they send their Lidef. We talk and come to an arrangement."

"What will you two be talking about?"

Jerren shifts uncomfortably.

Thomael stands with his son. "Judin, come with me. I would like to speak with you."

"No." Jerren stands now. Both are agitated. "Judin stays. She will know what has occurred."

I stand too and insert myself between my Mates. "What's occurred, Jerren?" It's my turn to flash a look to Thomael. "Sit down." I turn to Jerren and see Kinim take Leeiss from him. Our sons are sat in the play area, where they begin to crawl around. My Mates surround me, as Jerren continues.

"When you and Kinim were in town, you were Scented by an Ilestrian. We have not been told who it was, but your description has been given to them. They know Kinim is with you and that we are One. I've been asked to provide answers as to why you are on our world."

"You have to give them, don't you? For us?" I look to my other Mates and then back to Jerren. "Because I want to contribute to your society."

Thomael stomps forward and places his hands on my shoulders. "Our society. Yours and ours. We are one, too, min eurozan."

I turn under his hands. "Not yet we aren't, my love. I am

not yet fully like you, and that has put us all in danger." As I step to Jerren, I feel Thomael's hands slip from my shoulders. "What can I do to make this right, my soul? Do they want me? If it helps you all, they can take me and leave you all be."

Thomael growls loudly, and comes to stand directly behind my back. Kinim moves to take my hand, standing completely still beside me. Jerren's eyes storm over and I see the lightning in them.

"Giving you to them is not an option that I will allow. I will go to them first and try to help them see reasoning." He offers.

"And if they don't?" I ask, tilting my head toward my Mates. "If they want me and won't back down?"

"Then they will be no more." Thomael puts in coldly.

Kinim nods his head once. The same iciness shoots from his gaze to me and then to Jerren. "In the name of Judin, their people will burn. They will be a threat no longer."

I look to Jerren. His feral nature skirts the surface, as his gaze flicks to me and then to his other Becomings. "There have already been talks in Elorcui of Judin's heritage. Many are curious and asking questions, wanting answers. I've put them off as long as I can. I must go to the Ilestrians and try to help them see reasoning."

If the Ilestrian people don't see Jerren's reasoning, I know what will happen. As One, my Mates will burn everything of the Ilestrian to the ground. Men, women, and children would turn to dust, so that I would be kept safe. My Mates' possessive nature would convince them that it would be necessary to keep me. In the end, I would be responsible for their heartlessness.

"What if I wwere to go? Just me. Maybe I can help them see that I'm not a threat? That I just want to live with my Mates and our sons?" I implore to each of them, but it's no good. Not one of their faces gives me any hope.

"As soon as one of them saw you, they would capture you. No one would speak to you or hear your words. They would be allowed to do whatever they want to you, before bringing you to our frontete, our borders. Once the word spreads that you are there, they would declare you a visitor to this world and set your body on fire." Kinim said, not watching us but staring off to the side of where we stand.

Our sons fuss as Thomael charges at Kinim. "Stop it, K."

"Enough." Jerren's authoritative voice commands his earliest Becoming.

Thomael stops just before Kinim.

Kinim snaps out of his trance-like state and brings his eyes to me. "The only choice we have is for Jerren to speak with them."

"While I stay here, again, and wait to see if my soul comes back to me?" I wrap my arms around Jerren and look into his beautiful eyes. "Surely there is something I can do, min eurozan? I don't want to be passive anymore. I want a life – here – with all of you and our sons."

"You won't be passive, my dear." He leans out of my arms and takes my hands. "Paint, model, sculpt, and create. When all of this is said and done, you will have your area in the marketplace. You will take our sons with you and be accepted by all."

I want it so much to be true. "But how?"

"Because, as your Mates, we shall make it come to pass." Thomael moves to us and stands behind me, his hands landing softly on my shoulder.

"And because you will it, min eurozan. What you want often overrides what we see of our future. You have this way of making what you desire come to pass. We've never seen anyone like you." Kinim clasps my hand and comes close to me.

"I shall be home before you miss me, min eurozan." Jerren kisses me lightly. "And when I am home, we shall celebrate."

"Then I await your departure and your return." I kiss him back. "I love you, Jerren."

"And I you, Judin."

***

Four days later, my cycle has come to its end. Thomael steals me off to our room, so that he can be my first after almost a week of waiting anxiously. We both take turns mastering one another's senses and exit the room happily.

Kinim greets us with a smile and Jerren is joyous at the celebration of our love. Our sons meet us and together, as one, Lanon, Joeve, and Leeiss take their first steps. Our sons are growing so fast. Before we know it, they would be almost a year old. Time has gone by too fast.

The four of us fall back into our routine. There is a tenseness overshadowing in the household concerning Jerren's meeting with the Ilestrians.

The night before Jerren is to leave, I want to do something special for him. I have already asked Thomael and Kinim when Jerren would return, and they cannot give me a definite answer. So, I have sent Kinim to the marketplace with something to barter. I have an idea of what I want to do as a good-bye for my Mate. Kinim comes back with what I requested and I kiss him soundly, thanking him.

I made sure our sons are fed and my Mates slips off with them to the family room. When Jerren comes through the door from work, I greet him wearing just a couple of slips of the bright red cloth Kinim had admired. Our dinner is on the table. I would be his dessert.

"Min eurozan." Jerren sighs, admiring the simple ties that I have made with the cloth around my chest and waist. There isn't much material, but I don't think my Mate will mind.

"I want to give you a proper dinner and good-bye, before you go." I say, wrapping my arms around his neck and bringing him close for a deep kiss. "You are my soul. I'm going to need it later, and you now."

He sniffs loudly. "Is that my favorite meal?"

"Yep." I say, pulling him into the dining room. "And it is ready for us."

"What about our sons?" His eyes slide to the family room and then back to me. He already knows!

"Thomael and Kinim are with them, my love. Tonight is about you and me."

His hand grasps mine and we change course to the stairs.

"What are you doing? Dinner is going to get cold." Just before the stairs, he leans down to pick me up. "I'd prefer an appetizer before my meal, min eurozan. You shall be my hors d'oeuvre. I'm taking you to our room to gobble you up." His kiss to me is just as deep as the one I gave him

"What if I want to sample you, my love?" I ask, as he takes the stairs to our room. The door is already open and I am deposited on the bed.

"My warrior queen will be given every part of me. Every. Last. Drop." He sheds his clothes and joins me on our bed.

Several hours later, we sneak downstairs and all is dark. No sound comes from anywhere. Jerren is proudly marching around the house without anything on, while I am peeking around corners. I can't believe I agreed to walk around our house naked.

"I can't hear Thomael and Kinim speaking." I say, as Jerren heats our food.

We are halfway through our meal, when the dining room door opens, and my other two Mates bring in our sons.

"Good evening, Judin. Jerren." Kinim begins, presenting our son and Lanon to me. His kiss to me is quick. "Our sons are looking for a light repast and this is as perfect time as any to partake of it."

They bring them to me and our son begins nursing eagerly. "Thank you." I can't help the blush. When my Mates and I are individually sexually intimate, we have always washed and presented ourselves to the others. Jerren's essence and Scent is all over my body. I try to play it cool. "And what have my Mates and our sons been doing?"

Thomael scowls and then answers, staring at Lanon. "Spending much needed father time with our son." His answer was contrived, but his smile to our son is instantaneous.

Kinim smirks. "Enjoying the sounds of our bed knocking against the wall and banging on the floor."

My cheeks redden and I glance away from my Mates.

"Our Mate is getting rather adventurous in the bedroom." Jerren says, nonchalantly taking another bite of his food. "I'm enjoying all sides of her..." he paused, and my blush deepens, "personality."

"I'm glad you both are having a great time." Kinim takes a bite of the roast from the table. Joeve stops eating and Kinim takes him.

Thomael leans down to place his son in my arms. His lips capture mine in a hard kiss that leaves me reeling. He sits back down in his chair, but not before he grabs a piece of meat from the dish. "All that upstairs activity is making me hungry. Such energy being exerted."

Kinim throws him a nasty look. "Can you seriously not be happy? Our Mate is."

"I'm happy." Thomael says as Lanon detaches from my breast. "Come here, my son." He tries to snag Lanon from my arms, but I pull him close.

"I want to hold our son while I eat, my love." I continue on with my meal.

Kinim and Jerren chuckle lightly.

Thomael exits the room in a huff.

"I was spoiled back then. Rotten." Kinim muses. "I loved you, but I wanted my way, as often as I could get it." He leaves the table.

"I love you, Jerren, but you don't get your way all of the time, you know? I let you have it because I love you." I say, finishing my meal and pulling Lanon to me in a hug.

"I know you do." His hand covers mine. "Why don't you go find him and talk?"

"Because this night is about us, not Thomael."

Jerren's expression became serious. "It's about him too."

Kinim comes back with one of my gowns. "Here you go, Judin." He takes Lanon from my arms and hands him to Jerren. With one hand, he reaches out a hand and brings me to my feet. The gown slides over my head and he places a hand on my backside. "Go, and talk to your Mate. He needs you too."

"Okay." I move out of the dining room and see the front door standing wide open. Thomael is on the front steps of our home, looking up at the stars.

"I miss travelling with you. We had such excellent times." He muses, not looking at me.

"If you want to go, or need to go, then do it. I'm not going anywhere, and I will be here when you return." I move up behind him and bring my arms around his front, holding him close. "Always."

He is silent for a time. "I don't have their memories. I'm the first one. The first Becoming. They have mine. All of them. You and I have no moments of our own, not like they have with you."

"You're jealous." I didn't think it is possible of my Mates, but here it is.

"I'm not jealous of your Mates having you, I'm jealous of the memories that I'll never have with you. Kinim has all of my memories. Jerren has all of Jaad's and K's. If it's jealously to want our time together to be ours and not theirs, then I am a jealous Mate." He turns in my arms and brings his hands to my shoulders. "I know what it's like to kiss your mouth and touch you in the one spot that makes you lose yourself to me." His eyes bear into mine. "But so do they. Kinim and Jerren know how to please you better, because you and I have already done what we have."

"When Jerren said I was becoming more adventurous in our bedroom, it is because of you." I draw closer to him. "Our lovemaking may not just be our own, and, yes, you do have to share your memories with them, but you get to be my first.

You say you know where to touch me to lose myself because you found it first. When Kinim or Jerren do it, my body knows you were there first. You were the first one to claim it as your own. When they enter me, it's you, my body remembers. My heart may be with Kinim and my soul with Jerren, but my body remembers you. It's your touch I had first." I press my toes against the ground and kiss his lips. "Jerren may have my soul, as my Mate, and Kinim my heart, but you will always own my body. You know it, I know it, and it knows it."

"Mine." He grips my shoulders and drags me to him. His kiss is rough, demanding, and leaves me wanting more. The touch of his body to mine ignites a passion like none I have ever known. "Your body will always be mine."

"Forever," I breathe, as he draws me in for another kiss.

When we part, he slowly lets me go. "Jerren is wanting you again." He turns from me and looks back up at the stars.

"I will always be your forever," I say, slipping back through the door and back to the Mate I may not see for a while. I must make the most of our time together. For us.

CHAPTER EIGHTEEN
The Anomaly

*T*he morning dawns, and I awake to my Mates sleeping soundly in our bed. Kinim's arm is under my neck, Jerren's head is laying on my chest, and Thomael is breathing into the core of my being. The warm, bright sunsslight is streaming through the window.

I didn't want to move.

Jerren and I played together until we couldn't anymore last night. We showered, changed the sheets on the bed, and put on our robes. Our sons had already called it a night and were sleeping soundly. Thomael and Kinim were outside on the back concrete deck. Kinim was sitting in a chair and Thomael was laying down, both watching the stars.

The four of us made our way to the bedroom and my other two Mates readied themselves for the night. When they were finished, they laid down and one by one whispered a single phrase. "Min eurozan." Before long, all three of my Mates were sleeping soundly.

I am slowly becoming a new woman and a new species. A more assertive personality is gaining control of me.. Even my Mates are so in sync with one another, that they know when the other needs me, and allow me the precious time with them. Our sons are growing quickly, and would soon be more mobile.

Thomael's tongue surprises me, as it licks at my core. I moan. It is a move he does often during the night and early morning. I never question him about it. Maybe he wants me fresh on his tongue as he sleeps?

Kinim kisses the top of my head and pulls himself closer to me.

Jerren turns his head and opens his mouth to receive the fleshy goodness, that lies just under his cheek. After a couple of pulls, he lets go, sighs, and lays his head back down on my chest.

I note our sons, still sleeping in their cribs, and close my eyes to rest a while longer with my loves.

***

A single kiss to my lips. I work to chase the mouth that has given it. His lips are slightly roughened, the left bottom part of his lip is a little higher than the right. The moustache hair tickles my upper lip.

Not Jerren. His lower lip is fuller.

Another kiss. This one slightly more insistent, rounded fingertips touch my cheeks.

Ugh! My Mate is such a good kisser!

My mouth opens as his luscious tongue enters and we duel. His magnetism increases. Despite my activities with Jerren last night, between my Mates hands and tongue, I can be ready for him in a heartbeat.

This is my love. The one who can make me whole. And my love for him knows no bounds. Time and space can never keep us apart.

"Make love to me," I whisper, as he moves to lay on top of me.

I am ready for him, on the edge of losing myself to his touch.

"Please." I beg, as one of his hands move into my hair

and the other onto my thigh.

Not Thomael. Thomael always wraps my hair around his hand so he can control my movements to not only maximize my pleasure, but his.

"Min eurozan," I moan, as he withdraws from my touch.

I don't open my eyes as he readjusts himself to enter my body. His sculpted, rock hard body covers mine and I gasp.

Not Kinim. Kinim's body is tight, but it is narrower than the one on mine.

The lips feel wrong.

The touch is all wrong.

The body isn't one mine knows.

I open my eyes to see a beautiful pair of blue eyes staring back at me. Lust swirls in them, as they take me in. I have never seen the face above me in my entire life.

My heart slams against my chest and my core throbs, aching to be filled with the man above me. The one whose very self is ready to make me his own. I feel him at the center of my being.

I scream and begin to move out from under him, but he traps me beneath his large body.

"Min eurozan?" His voice is filled with concern, and love. "Are you alright, my love?"

"Let me up!" I try moving again, and this time he releases me.

I scoot off of the bed and as I do, I grab the sheet to cover myself. "Who are you? What do you want?"

The man on the bed, correction: the Elorcuian, as I can smell his Scent, on the bed sits up without covering himself. Every inch of him looks to be sculpted from marble. If I was into how a man looks, I would be all over that.

But I'm not. My life is my Mates and our sons. This Elorcuian has no right to defile our bed with his presence.

"Get off of our bed this instant!" I spit at him. "That is our place and it is sacred." My hair flies around my face in anger. I want to rake my nails across his face and draw blood.

"Where are my Mates?"

He lifts his nose to bring in my Scent. "I do love it when we are in bed and you are angry. It makes you more tempting." His feet hit the floor and he strides up to me, resting his hands on my shoulders. A very Thomael move, all cocky and arrogant. Self-assured of what is his.

"I'm not tempting to you. I can't be." I rail at him and draw back from his touch.

"But you are, min eurozan. I need you badly." His fingertips touch my cheek. It's a Kinim move. He looks down at himself and then to me. "See how much I want to make love to you?"

I back away from him, uncertain. My body responds to his touch, as if it already knows it. My heart feels secured to his. My mind knows his intellect. Our souls feel connected. "Where is Thomael, Kinim and Jerren?" I ask, looking around the room. "Who are you?"

His charcoal eyebrows dip and his blue eyes harden just a bit. Confusion lights them. "I am Thomael and Kinim, Judin."

My mouth drops, as he continues.

"I don't know who Jerren is. Is he one of my next Becomings?" He starts to move closer to me, but I back up.

"Jerren came after Jaad. It was Thomael then Kinim then Jaad and Jerren. They are my loves. I sleep with them every night and wake with them every morning." I step around the mountain of Elorcuian in front of me. "Where are they?"

He crosses his thick arms, corded with more muscles than I can count. "I am your Mate. I am Roenn. I Became after Kinim. Do you not remember my Becoming?"

Did I miss something? Ugh!

No! I would remember the Becoming of this Mate. If one was to take an image of Thomael, Kinim, Jaad, and Jerren and blur them together and create a new image, it would be the one in front of me. "Roenn?"

"Yes." He uncrosses his arms and takes a step before me.

I hold out a hand. "What was the nature of your

Becoming?"

"My thousand years were up as Kinim. We were in love, so I chose to Become. For you." He gestures to the front of himself. "A step up from Thomael and Kinim, don't you think?" Thomael's arrogance. Again.

I don't look down. I know what I would see. My mind and heart, every molecule of every cell of my body, would tell me he is mine and I am his.

But it's a lie! I know myself. I don't know this person in front of me.

"It doesn't matter what I think." What my body, heart, mind, and soul thinks, I add silently. "I don't know you. Where is Jerren?"

"You keep mentioning this 'Jerren'." He air quotes my love's name. "I don't know a 'Jerren'."

I stop, trying not lose it.

Instead, I focus my panic on the Elorcuian in front of me. "Your name is Roenn?"

He nods his exceptionally handsome head and the coal black hair falls over his sinfully blue eyes.

"And you are the Becoming after Kinim?"

Another nod and the hair at the nape of his neck slides just over the thick muscles of his shoulders.

"How did your Becoming begin?"

"You were in my office. Kinim had brought you to me, so that once I Became, we could be together." Answering my question as if speaking to a small child.

"Why was I in your office?" I ask, carefully.

"Because Thomael and Kinim wanted you as theirs. Bringing you to me was a logical step in keeping you as ours." He says, smoothly, crossing his ankles. The muscles in his thighs snaked seductively.

Don't fan yourself. He isn't yours! And you don't want him.

My core throbbed in denial. "You all didn't think I would have a say in being on a new world in a city that isn't my own?" I ask, staring straight into baby blues.

Baby blues! Tears spring to my eyes! Our sons!

I whirl to see the screens active and our sons beginning to rouse. "Our sons! Do you remember me being pregnant in your office with our sons?"

He turns his head slightly to the screens and his mouth drops. "Babies." His feet move across the room and out the door.

I follow him, dropping the sheet when he's too fast for me to keep up. Motherly instincts kick in and I make it to the nursery before him. "Wait!" A hand and foot comes to each side of the door frame.

"Whose children are those?" He questions, taking my shoulders in his hands and trying to move me out of the way.

"Mine!" I wrap my legs around his torso and hold on to his neck with my arms. "They are all mine. Don't you dare touch them!"

All movements from him stop when I come flush with his body. "Min eurozan." He lifts his head and kisses me soundly.

"Stop that!" I yell, wanting to hit him in his handsome face. "You're not my Mate!"

"I'm not your Mate?" Rejection and pain slam me in the gut.

I feel what he is experiencing. I've hurt him.

"I'm not your Mate." He turns to stagger to the floor and lands with a thud. "Why do I feel as if I own you? I know your taste in my mouth, how you feel in my hands and when I am in your body. How can I know every inch of your skin with my bare hands, without ever touching you?" His eyes find mine. "Every cell in my body is screaming that I am yours, yet you say I am not? When did your heart change, Judin? Do you not love me as your min eurozan anymore?"

I never, in a thousand years, no pun intended, ever, thought I would be sitting on the floor next to one of the most gorgeous men I have never met, at the door of three children who weren't his, but were, and telling him that he wasn't my

Mate. It all sounded surreal and unbelievable.

Yet, here I was. Our sons: mine, Thomael, Kinim, and Jerren's are behind the nursery door, ready to receive myself and their fathers. Fathers who are not here, but I am. And, if Roenn is actually their father, wouldn't he remember them?

How could a father not know his own son? If he is Thomael and Kinim, wouldn't he feel a connection to his sons?

I look to Roenn, but don't note his features. Because I have seen him once, I can describe him down to the curly haired vee that leads to the center of his body. "Do you not feel anything for our sons?" I glance to the door and then back to him.

He copies my motion and then holds my eyes with his. "I have no memory of the babies, Judin." His feet come to the floor and he brings his elbows to his knees. His hands come to his hair. "In my heart, you are my Mate, and I know you, but I don't know the boys behind that door."

My heart drops in my chest. This is all wrong!

"I do not mean to hurt you, my love." He crouches down on all fours and gracefully begins to moves toward me.

I allow him to come a few feet away, then hold up my hand. "Stop!"

"But you are hurting." He brings his hands off of the floor and kneels. "I don't want to see you hurt. Ever."

"Don't say that." I remember Jaad saying those exact words. "Those are his words, Roenn. Stop using their words on me."

"But they are true." Sincere honesty rings true in his words.

"Is this an Ilestrian sent to trick and deceve me, or are you really one of my Mates?"

About the Author

Cathy Jackson is a Midwestern Christian mother of two twenty-somethings and two teenagers. Reading is a passion of hers, but she adores writing. Some of the best people have been placed in her life to help her publish her books. They are a blessing and mean more to her than they will ever know. She loves writing scenes that uplift and encourage along with making one feel the experience. She wants readers to finish the books feeling hope, love, and happiness. To date, the books she has published are Inspirational (Christian) Romances but they have a Contemporary Romance feel.

www.ingramcontent.com/pod-product-compliance
Lightning Source LLC
Chambersburg PA
CBHW020651260626
47157CB00008B/2984